The Master

THE FRENCH LIST

PATRICK RAMBAUD

The Master

TRANSLATED BY
NICOLE BALL AND DAVID BALL

LONDON NEW YORK CALCUTTA

This work is published with the support of the
Publication Assistance Programmes of the
Institut français

Seagull Books, 2023

First published in French as *Le Maître* by Patrick Rambaud
© Editions Grasset & Fasquelle, Paris, 2015

First published in English translation by Seagull Books, 2023
English translation © Nicole Ball and David Ball, 2023

ISBN   978 1 8030 9 062 7

British Library Cataloguing-in-Publication Data
A catalogue record for this book is available from the British Library

Typeset by Seagull Books, Calcutta, India
Printed and bound by WordsWorth India, New Delhi, India

To Tieu Hong, my darling.

*To Professors Jean-François Billeter
and Jean Levi, my guides.*

*To Jean-Paul Milou, my enduring Master
at Lycée Condorcet.*

Since everything lies open to view,
there is nothing to explain.

Ludwig Wittgenstein

CHAPTER ONE

How Zhuang Fell Upon Our Earth

It was twenty-five centuries ago in the land of Song, between the Yellow River and the River Huai. Zhuang Zhou was born without a cry, with his eyes wide open. Since newborns resemble old people, he too appeared crumpled, toothless and bald—men enter the scene as defenceless as they leave it. In Chinese lands, the first cry constitutes the individual, for the soul expresses itself by breath, but Zhuang Zhou had not cried: he only smiled at the lacquered beams of the ceiling. Aware of the anomaly, his mother wanted to get a closer look at him. She had herself carried over to him and stared at him with horror in her eyes. She had cried out instead. 'This hideous tadpole is a demon,' murmured the mother, and then, falling back with her mouth open, breathed her last in the arms of her servants.

Without even taking account of the tragedy, the music master, the cook and a soothsayer first conformed to the ritual: they were in place of the father who was forbidden to see his wife three months before and after childbirth. The men wondered if the too-joyful child was respecting the conventions.

'But the child cried out! I heard him!' said the music master, who was blind.

'The cry was the cry of his poor mother.'

'What about him?'

'He's mocking us,' said the cook, nervously shaking his bamboo-bark fan.

'When you come out of the warm womb of your mother and fall into the world of men, there's nothing to laugh about.'

'Perhaps he's an idiot.'

'Before he can even speak?'

'Let us study his case,' said the soothsayer, adjusting the cord of his hat. 'Did you notice an omen?'

'None,' the cook answered.

'A spectacular storm just before his birth, with thunder and lightning?' the soothsayer continued.

'You know very well there hasn't been a drop of rain since the fifth moon.'

'An eagle circling over the roof?'

'Not even a sparrow.'

'What about a celestial apparition we could maybe pretty up? A dragon at his mother's bedside?'

'Those are fables to be invented later,' said the music master.

They agreed on covering up the ill-starred event, going out on the doorstep and shooting arrows in the air to hail the arrival of a boy, as if everything were happening according to the laws of nature. They could not let the neighbours gossip, spread rumours, talk of some miracle or sorcery; they had to make sure the baby didn't arouse jealousy. The three of them leaned over the newborn who was full of vitality, arms and legs thrashing the air, showing he was happy to be alive. They drew nearer, crawling on all fours to observe him better. The infant thought he was attacked by evil spirits: he took fright at those stern faces, the milky eyes of the music master, the scattered hairs on the soothsayer's chin, the crooked stumps in the cook's mouth, so he began to scream and he screamed so loudly that they all breathed a sigh of relief: 'At last! He howled like the wind!' These honourable men threatened the servants into silence: all was normal, they had seen nothing and heard nothing; they could explain to the heartbroken father that his wife died while giving birth to the little one, without telling him the real reason, because they couldn't possibly accuse such a tender little pipsqueak of causing her death. Life resumed its ordinary, sad, secret course.

In winter, the peasants would re-enter the ramparts of the cities, pile into clay shacks and eat boiled nettle stems. They had no names. On orders, this anonymous mass went from working in the fields to military duties. Zhou had a family name, Zhuang, and that is what we'll call him from now on. This name was the prerogative of nobles, said the father who claimed to be descended from a king of Song, but in reality he belonged to the new class of functionaries that was emerging at the end of the feudal era. After uniting the vassals under their authority, the local princes now ruled over a vaster territory and moved away from the country people to shut themselves inside their capitals. This marked a change in the traditions of the villages. Society was growing complicated. Born from new needs, the intermediary class was beginning to assert itself: from the steward to the copyist, educated scribes who knew the ten thousand signs of

Chinese writing were becoming indispensable in order to administrate and oversee the region.

On wooden tablets bound together with thongs, they wrote administrative documents with hare-fur brushes. Their influence grew from year to year in keeping with their knowledge, their evolving lifestyles and their glibness. They took advantage of this to rise above the others and emerged as the dominant caste.

Zhuang's father, Zhou, was a kind of steward for the prince in the city of Mong. For a time, he watched over the public granaries, retaining people through favours but also provoking lasting grudges. Then he profited from his sovereign's benevolence and was promoted to Superintendent of Gifts and Presents. The position was much envied. From then on, he would distribute funds to whomever he fancied and took care to bribe the entourage of other princes by sending them money, dancers or concubines. Corruption had become a principle of government that even extended to private interests. Zhou could corrupt a judge or mollify a rival by offering him a troupe of loose, tame young women.

Each time a dusty chariot with drawn curtains arriving from afar stopped before the Superintendent's house, craftsmen, shopkeepers, foremen, officers, kids and old people would all crowd silently against the painted, lacquered columns of the entrance to catch a glimpse of the new girls—Chinese or Barbarian girls coated with scented herbs who would soon be offered or sold. Mr. Zhou was satisfied with these graceful deliveries; he made no mystery of his venerable profession.

Zhuang remembered his early years so badly that he never spoke of them. He lived cossetted in the north wing of the paternal home, in the women's pavilion. He had no mother, but there were forty of them; it was a privilege. He grew up among a swarm of sisters, cousins and aunts, but also in permanent contact with the harem of dancers and concubines that was continually replenished. He was every woman's toy and each one showered a different kind of tenderness on him They could see themselves in his eyes better than in their bronze mirrors, so much did he admire their rings and metal bracelets, the headbands that held back their smooth hair, the figures of their embroideries where he learned mythology, the wide pants they put on under their split tunics whose colours followed the rhythm of the seasons, red in summer, white in autumn . . . Zhuang also knew that vinegar mutton heralded the spring, and in winter, a wind loaded with yellow sand would blow and veil the countryside.

From this generous period, he had no unpleasant memories, except for his first bath, when he almost drowned. Zhuang was only a month old. The whole family, friends from the provinces and dignitaries had come to see him splash around in a small pool decorated with pieces of brilliant cloth. They tossed hazelnuts and gold coins in the warm, perfumed water for good luck. The women were stirring the bathwater with their hairpins. Zhuang had slipped out of the hands that held him and disappeared into the pool for a few seconds. The water entered through his mouth, ears and eyes, but he was quickly returned to the surface, where he threw a fit that witnesses smilingly attributed to fear. The ultimate humiliation: they shaved his head and kept a few strands of his hair in a box. A few years later, they tonsured him again, leaving only a tuft of hair sticking up like a brush on the top of his head, making Zhuang distrustful of water and barbers throughout his entire life.

By the age of five, he had to leave the world of women to suddenly discover the world of men and the hellish realm of ritual. For a long time, he missed the muffled giggles of his many playmates, the rustling of silk, their curves when they danced, the tinkling of the little bells they wore about their ankles, the velvet of their voices, and their moist eyes when they cradled him in their arms.

CHAPTER TWO

The Ghosts of Song

Young Zhuang finally got to explore the house he'd been living in. It seemed enormous to the child's eyes. The projecting upper stories, the double galleries, the fence around the inner courtyard, the windows covered with wooden lattice—everything was shut, rigid, silent. Silhouettes in black robes with lambswool lining and bonnets hanging low over their foreheads slipped in and out of the curtains of the high-ceilinged rooms. The ladies took off their luxurious garments and wore austere clothing when they went into town, to ward off envy. Here, human beings seemed to shrink, transparent as the ghosts that filled the rooms and the bending corridors with their presence, for the ancestors floated around them and were more alive than the living; they were only spoken of in a hushed voice, animals were sacrificed in their honour on specific dates, with belled knifes and ritual gestures. The names of the family dead swung on tablets over the ancestors' altars, and bronze vases and little dishes filled with magic signs were arranged in an immutable order.

Zhuang was learning to speak by imitation: he could recite the words of the ceremonies but was mostly interested in the flies that fluttered around the offal of the victims; his gaze followed them and flew off in turn towards the overhanging roofs. The incense tickled his throat and the gongs, cymbals and fifes sustained his submission to the ghosts. He assiduously frequented the ectoplasm of his grandfather, whom he knew only in this vaporous form.

He had no feelings for his father and as there was no such thing as childhood, his father had none for him. Zhuang just followed the rules with docility. To obey was a lesser evil. Falling asleep on his mat at night, he would pull his wolfskin blanket up to his eyes; only then, in the dark, could he find some calm. His two brothers woke him before dawn, and he would see the elder turn into a servitor as he put on his ceremonial costume to present delicacies to Chou, who had his back oriented in the traditional position to the north of his large bedroom. The brother would then wash Chou's face with rice water and wipe his spit and snot. Prohibitions restricted life. The sons did not have the right to take the stairs reserved for their father, they must never touch his clothes or his pillow, nor the stool he leaned on, nor his stick. They did not have the right to cough, yawn or scratch their buttocks. Fortunately, Zhuang was the youngest son, and his mission was to hunt down dust with his dog-hair broom. He performed this mechanical task while dreaming, for he had learnt to escape through thought.

In the morning scramble, as the elder brother was hurrying to be on time to wash their father's face, he accidentally stepped on Zhuang's foot.

'Ow!'

'Be quiet!' said the big brother as he buttoned up his robe illustrated with formulas.

'You hurt me!'

'Nonsense! Me, I didn't feel a thing!'

'But I did!'

Faced with his brother's indifference, as he followed along the halls limping, Zhuang had the first rational thought of his boyhood, a way of reasoning he would develop years later: 'I say *me*, he says *me*, we speak the same way but we're saying the opposite.' What's the point of explaining oneself when you can't reconcile opposing points of view? Putting aside this argument, Zhuang kept quiet during the ceremony. As he watched his brother washing their father, always with the same gestures in the same order, he resolved never to complain about anything, since everyone was utterly indifferent to how he felt. When it rained hard, he did not wail like the others, 'What did I do to Heaven to deserve this downpour?' He simply watched the water dripping down the roofs into a bamboo bucket. He resolved never to feel hot or cold and realized that by not thinking about it any more he was able to feel less hot or less cold. Whether in frigid weather or in the scorching heat he would keep laughing and frolicking about just the same.

And so, through rain or wind, Zhuang left every morning to study in a school next door to the palace of Duke Wu. There he'd learn manners, submission and archery with the offspring of the prominent members of society. Together with the other boys, he spent hours repeating the lines of Confucius on filial piety and order:

'The Master says, The good man is level-headed and magnanimous, the man of little worth is always agitated and perplexed.'

'The Master says, Noblemen with no humanity can sometimes be found, but a man of little worth full of humanity, never.'

The examples Zhuang had already stored in his short life seemed to prove the falsity of the sage's maxims. Who were the men of little worth? Had he encountered any? Yes. When he walked through the village of Mong to his classes, he would run into such men. They looked mulish, sullen and remained silent, completely engrossed in their chores. He saw peasants requisitioned to build new earthen walls to the sound of a drum. They were gagged and Zhuang wondered why. So nobody could hear them protest? Probably. Then how could you know what they thought of the Duke of Song? He also walked in front of the great gate where swarms of crows were tearing apart the bodies of condemned men who had been hanged there. Shopkeepers were driving away the birds with sticks to cut strips of meat off the corpses, which they would then soak in brine and sell in the market. Zhuang had a flashing thought: 'Was the gazelle created for the tiger?' Does the man of little worth exist only to be crushed?

In a few years, Zhuang learnt a great deal from his masters and from the whispered conversations he had at night with the spirit of his departed grandfather. He did not make friends with the sons of the rich, well-fed officials with whom he studied politeness and rituals. He merely observed them. To him they were hypocrites, putting on serious faces or feigning enthusiasm as they recited Confucius. Beneath their refined appearance, at the age when young humans turn into brutes, Zhuang thought them capable of the ruses necessary for someone who wants to hold on to his position in the world, with utter disregard for friends and neighbours. He kept his distance. The other boys took that for timidity, stupidity or indifference. In their company, however, he learnt that the earth was square and heaven wrapped above it like a canopy, swallows turned into shellfish in early autumn, sparrows into oysters and quail into field mice. One had to believe everything without ever seeing any of it happen. Doubt was confusedly hatching in his heart.

When his masters told him of the Barbarians who were pressing against the confines of the Chinese kingdoms, his doubt was reinforced. They dressed in straw, the masters said, and the Jongs in animal skins wore bramble hats; in the East lived men with tattooed bodies who devoured raw meat, and in the North, where not one tree grew, the Ti people dressed in feathers and slept in caves. Zhuang believed that the masters were talking about vagrants from the time of Confucius, two centuries ago. He knew all these different tribes were now assimilated. He had lived alongside magnificent Barbarians in the women's pavilion in his early childhood. They were pretty, knowledgeable, perfumed, and they gave their bodies up to the dance unrestrainedly; they strummed the seven strings of the black-lacquered zithers to surround you with languor. Zhuang kept silent and acted docile so as to be left in peace. When he walked up on the terrace overlooking the city, his gaze wandered over the countryside; he would be intoxicated by the clusters of flowers hidden under large catalpa leaves, stirred by the dark green of the cypresses, by the mist that erased the low hills and lingered over the moors. He wanted to know how people lived far away, beyond those forests of blue mulberry trees. The land of Song seemed to him frozen in the past.

By the age of ten, Zhuang had grasped the foundation of Chinese thought, which was based on simple principles. 'Yes' and 'no' did not exist in a natural state. There were no contradictions, only contrasts; the world was a sum of impressions. Complementary forces combined, followed each other, switched around, joined together, harmonized and replaced each other, like Yin and Yang, night and day, darkness and light, woman and man. Life was constantly evolving, nothing was definitive. What constituted the existence of men, animals and things was always in motion. Yin needed Yang and Yang needed Yin, in order for balance to be maintained.

Writing allowed Zhuang to get an inkling of this idea of balance. His education was rough and boring at first: for a long time, he had to practice like a dancer who forces himself through gymnastics and pain to gain flexibility, or like a musician who loosens his fingers by endlessly repeating staffs of notes. Squatting in front of a low table, he applied himself to the ceremonial. Holding the brush vertically, its wolf hair saturated with black ink, Zhuang practiced tracing the three hundred sixty-four essential characters, letting only his wrist do the work. The movement became smoother as he went along. He reproduced the characters stored in his memory like choreography, the ten characters of 'horse', the seventeen of 'turtle'. Dots, curves, bars—he learnt to associate them to expand his vocabulary. When his mind and body finally fused, when his forearm traced the signs without his having to think about them, when he could set ideas or things on a tablet with a brush stroke, he realized he knew how to write.

'Now,' said his father, 'You can become a government official.'

CHAPTER THREE

At the Court of Wu-the-Morose

Chou asked for an audience before the Duke of Song to present his son, whose writing possessed elegance. Zhuang studied how to walk, turn, walk backwards while remaining vertical, but also how to bow naturally, without bending too much or too little, almost at a right angle; the boy practiced a hundred times before he obtained a satisfactory curve. They shoved a pearled cap on his skull, fitted him with a custom-made tunic with rounded sleeves hemmed with wild dog's fur so he could make charming gestures with his hands. Zhuang was ready when the great day arrived, and, exceptionally, he had the right to climb onto the paternal palanquin. He expected to meet a considerable personage, the wisest of the men of Song, an emperor of mythical times venerated by his masters, equal to Yao-the-Great in virtue. That sovereign lived long ago in a palace with rough-hewn beams and mostly ate mashed millet seeds; he wore rough canvas clothes with a deerskin cape over them when it was cold; Yao detested the superfluous, and so he lived in people's memories as a perfect, exemplary emperor. People forgot about his wars and the way he had of cutting his enemies into slices.

Before he even met the Duke of Song, Zhuang understood he would not resemble Yao-the-Great: once he went through the finely carved wooden door of the palace, the luxury he discovered there was a complete surprise. He looked at the terraced rows of silvery cedar trees, raised his eyes to the huge tiled roofs, admired the covered galleries, the plumed horses with gilded bits that uniformed grooms were leading by the bridle. Guided by a chamberlain in a white fox coat, father and son walked majestically through rooms filled with gigantic, bright-coloured statues. Now rugs were deadening their steps. Zhuang began to count the motionless guards, terrifying in their metal helmets, their tiger skins and those halberds they all held exactly the same way. 'Our duke is protected,' Zhuang said to himself, 'There are two hundred and twenty-four of them just in the corridors.' Then he wanted to stop and admire a carillon of fifty little bronze bells that were swinging to and fro in a lacquered wooden frame, but his father set him in motion again with a discrete dig of the elbow.

When Chamberlain Sun opened the seventh door for them, Zhuang finally saw Wu-the-Morose, Duke of Song, hunched in a square armchair on top of a flight of stairs. He was a wizened old man with a waxy complexion and hollow cheeks, whose nose and chin met like pliers. His fringed bonnet prevented him from seeing, his yellow silk ear flaps prevented him from hearing: thus did he protect himself from the world. On his clothing were embroidered the three insignias of his rank: the mountain, the dragon and the pheasant. Without these images that identified him, he could have been taken for one of those rag dolls people buy at the fair. He was surrounded by petrified astrologers and servants; one of them bent over double to bring him swan's blood in a jade cup: he downed it in one gulp before making a gesture with his wrist that the chamberlain interpreted as he usually did:

'Mighty Lord, here is your Superintendent of Pleasures and his son.'

'Mmm . . . ,' said the noble duke.

The astrologers whispered as they observed Zhuang.

'This little boy cuts a fine figure,' suddenly said a big voice coming out of a little body.

Song-Kou was the prince's buffoon, a hunchbacked dwarf who grimaced and deformed his mouth while moving his ears.

'Do you intend to replace our duke?' the chamberlain asked, half-jokingly.

'Sometimes I do, Venerable Sun, sometimes I do. Today I made him laugh twice and that gives me rights till this evening.'

Song-Kou was exaggerating his role as an entertainer, but his contortions authorized him to utter serious things in a light-hearted way. He rose from the step he was sitting on, walked crab-like towards Zhuang and turning to the duke, declared:

'He could watch over the palace kitchens, since he has decent handwriting, and do the accounts of our provisions. I noticed that some of them tend to vanish.'

'Mmm,' said Wu-the-Morose again.

'Our Wonderful Prince gave his agreement!' To the visitor, 'What is your name?'

'Zhuang Zhou.'

'I will personally explain your work to you. I know everything they cook in this palace *better than a soothsayer.*'

Song-Kou gave a comic bow to the astrologers and to Chamberlain Sun.

To consecrate his younger son's entry into the court, Chou dragged him to a temple where they prostrated themselves before the shell of a tortoise; the characters carved on it meant *happiness*. 'What good does it do him to be a relic?' thought Zhuang, as he imagined the animal splashing around happily in a pond. He remembered the stories his aunt Feng used to tell him when he was living in the women's quarters, particularly the one about the sea bird that landed on Lu pond. The duke was hunting in the area, saw it and was enchanted: what ease, what plumage, what grace, he said to himself, and he ordered his soldiers to capture it. A captain skilled at throwing a net caught the bird alive. It hardly struggled in the mesh. The duke took it in his hands to admire it. The bird was no longer singing and its eyes were blank. The duke carried it to his carriage and brought it to the temple of the ancestors to celebrate it. Musicians played a melody that failed to charm it; they sacrificed a cow to give it back its energy. Nothing helped. The bird remained dreamy. Back at the palace, the duke had meat and wine served up to it, but the bird did not touch anything. It died of starvation in three days.

'They should have given it birdseed,' said aunt Feng.

'And let it fly away,' said Zhuang.

'You know, child, princes make as many blunders with their people as they do with seabirds.'

Sometimes, the story was told differently, depending on the teller. A wretched peasant would then replace the seagull. Guards dragged him to the palace, he was offered a silken bed as if to check some kind of experiment and then served dishes too delicate for him, an eater of roots and pea leaves. They replaced his hempen clothes with fine linens. The peasant couldn't take it. He fell ill. The moral of this new story was that everyone should rot away in his own assigned place. Confucius did not teach anything different.

CHAPTER FOUR

Of Broth and Men

Zhuang found himself in the pantry of the palace along with two young rogues who were, like him, apprentice officials, but at fifteen he was the youngest. As he had promised, the dwarf Song-Kou ticked off his tasks before leaving him in the company of the two other scribes. Together, they were to check the entry of merchandise and make sure they were properly used, so the produce would not get lost or eaten or resold by the kitchen boys and the whole battery of sous-chefs who specialized in the confection of one dish or another, or in one method of cooking or another.

'You're lucky Song-Kou is protecting you,' said the first scribe.

'But you won't take advantage of it in his absence,' said the second.

'How's that?'

'Here, you must see nothing. You must be silent and pretend.'

'Pretend what?' asked Zhuang.

The three boys were sitting behind writing-cases at the entrance of the goods they were to check off. The first scribe explained:

'When a merchant comes in with his load, he shouts, "Three hundred quail!" and you write down *three hundred quail*. You don't have the time to check, it goes by too fast, and the clerks seize the rest immediately—theoretically so as not to waste time, in fact to misappropriate some.'

'That's right,' said the second scribe, 'Some quails never reach our ovens. They're stolen.'

'By the store clerks?'

'By everyone,' said the first.

'Everyone profits from it,' said the second, 'And so do we.'

'It's theft!' said Zhuang indignantly.

'Yes, but it's been well organized for ages, and nobody realizes it in the palace.'

'After all,' said the second scribe, 'It's part of our job as officials—to close our eyes and be rewarded for it . . . '

'Confucius says . . .' Zhuang began.

'Confucius can say whatever he likes,' the first scribe interrupted.

'We're the ones in true reality,' the second insisted.

Zhuang blamed himself for his sententious tone; he didn't know he could talk like that and it surprised him. 'What right do I have,' he thought, 'To preach to these two silly boys?'

Guided by his associates, in a few days Zhuang grew familiar with the atmosphere of the kitchens, long rooms that took up the whole basement of the palace pierced with narrow latticed openings to evacuate the smells, the smoke from the torches and the steam. When he arrived, he inspected the vats of boiling water where carps were blanching, soon to be finely minced, basins of fresh water where fat-bellied river fish were swimming around, waiting to be fried, steaming cauldrons, flames from fireplaces where freshly killed tortoises would be roasted, and the frog well. Everywhere food was being cooked, cut, sliced, gutted, grilled, boiled or sizzled. The faces of the kitchen boys were glowing. Around a table, children were stuffing ant eggs into duck tongues with their little fingers. Near them, helpers sliced up caramelized pigs with a cleaver, steamed dogs under a bed of bitter herbs, roasted cranes, rectified chick broth or a soup of wild geese. Magpies marinated in large earthenware jars. A sous-chef was stir-frying breams with an expert hand while his colleagues chopped a fawn into slivers or scorched hummingbirds to be crunched in one mouthful.

The times were ferocious, but the cuisine, refined.

Every day, the palace chef would come and order the dishes for the prince, his ministers, his counsellors, even the guests he needed to cajole; he distributed the tasks and entrusted their execution to his assistants, who followed him with servility.

'Watch out!' said the first scribe, 'He's coming.'

Immediately, the three officials plunged their noses into their tablets and pretended to count the boxes of pheasants the porters were presenting to them. Chef Tse Kao walked past them without a glance. He had a bored look, a scornful mouth, and walked with small steps, pushing his considerable paunch before him. His head nodding gently between the kettles and the vats, he vaguely waved his horsehair flyswatter.

'I recognize him,' whispered Zhuang. 'It's the Prime Minister.'

'Here, he's the chef,' answered the second scribe.

'He's Prime Minister *too*?'

'He's Prime Minister because he's the chef.'

In the fourth century before our era, holding these two functions concurrently seemed natural. The man who could come up with a perfectly balanced broth could bring harmony between men. He represented measure, he knew exactly how to adapt the cooking to the product, he also knew that tastes develop in tune with colours and consistencies, which had to be combined with subtlety. Tse-Kao visited his kitchens in the morning and reserved his afternoons for the current affairs of Song, which consisted in establishing submissive, peaceful relations with powerful neighbours, much more voracious than his little country. Unfortunately for Song, its soil was fertile and excited their greed, so conflicts and any occasion for conflict had to be avoided. Tse-Kao had the same practices with the other princes as he did with the ancestors and evil spirits. He never left the basement kitchens before offerings were prepared. He asked for plump animals for the sacrifice. Never, he would say, poke fun at the spirits that surround us. These spirits were many, mischievous and easily offended. They must be prevented from harming us. They demanded offerings of quality and that was enough to content them; let's prevent them from provoking epidemics to take their revenge for a petty sacrifice, that's all we ask. That's why they were represented on the altars in their best light. That big fish illustrated the god of the river, and that bird with a deer's head the god of the wind; a smiling toad symbolized the master of rain, to whom prayers were offered during dry spells, just in case. All that was simply bargaining and superstition. Religions had not yet contaminated China.

'Tse-Kao collects the sacrificed animals. You should see how greedily he gobbles them up,' the first scribe said to Zhuang when the chef had left.

'And we get to eat what's left of the feast,' said the second scribe. 'That Tse-Kao sure is a glutton! You should see him plunging his hand into the fried grasshoppers, tearing apart the meat with his canines. With his chin shining with sauces, he's in ecstasy, I swear.'

'It makes him belch with pleasure.'

'What about the spirits?' asked Zhuang.

'For him, they don't exist.'

'His world is reduced to the roundness of his paunch.'

'How can he rule over the country,' Zhuang continued, 'if he's only interested in the size of his belly?'

'Good question!' the two rogues said, laughing.

Zhuang remembered Confucius saying you had to learn all the time and above all have the desire to learn. The palace kitchens gave him a terrain for varied observations—amusing or instructive. The Old Master's teaching enabled him to withstand his utterly uninteresting work as a bookkeeper. He showed perfect neutrality in his interactions with men and things, which he put in the same boat, accepting the breaking of a bowl or his co-workers' thefts without turning a hair, but he remained curious about everything. As soon as he could steal a little rest on some pretext or other, he would question the sous-chefs about their practices. It was in this way that he learnt the peculiar alimentary habits of Duke Wu-the-Morose who wanted to be close to nature but demanded refinements that moved him away from it. He had decided that the kitchen boys should intervene as little as possible in preparing his meals and let nature do most of the work. They twisted themselves into knots to obey him.

'How are you managing with this order?' Zhuang asked a sous-chef assigned to the prince's private meals.

'You see this load of coconuts?'

'Well sure! A hundred of them came in this morning. I see them, but I also see they're smeared with signs.'

'It's so we know when the frogs are ready.'

'What frogs?'

'The frogs we stuff them with, of course. When they're little, we put a frog in each nut, through a tiny hole we fill in again very quickly with a perforated piece of wood so they can't escape. Inside, the prisoner drinks the milk and eats the flesh of the coconut. And then it fattens up. The day comes—a day we know how to calculate—when the frog has eaten and drunk the whole contents of the nut. We say it's ready to be eaten. It seems the grilled legs of this animal are delicious when they're exclusively flavoured with coconut.'

'You tasted some of them?'

'Oh, no! This delicacy is reserved for our prince.'

Another time, the sous-chef told him how carps would get stuffed all by themselves to the great delight of Duke Wu. They were dipped into a basin of cold water and fistfuls of finely chopped aromatic herbs were thrown into it. The carp swallowed everything that floated on the water's surface when the basin was put over the fire, and the fish slowly cooked while stuffing itself greedily. The Prime Minister preferred what he called 'drunken carp'. It meant plunging the body of the fish, but not the head, into a very hot bath of frying oil, and immediately serving the fried animal with its mouth still alive and trying to breathe, while they poured millet wine into it. 'You can't imagine a fresher dish!' the Prime Minister would exclaim, leaving only the bones of his victim on the plate.

What attracted Zhuang's attention more seriously was the way Master-Butcher Ling cut up carcasses of beef. He was a slight man with white hair and long musician's fingers. He would stand motionless in front of the steer hanging before him, watch it to make sure its presence was real, take a deep, slow breath, and his eyes would go blank. Then Ling would grab the carcass with his left hand and wedge it against his shoulder and his bent knee. Then his sharp knife began working. Only him and this knife could be seen dancing, as if hand and arm were following him by tracing arabesques in the air. He looked like a dancer according his movements to the rhythm of the 'Lynx Head', that old traditional song. His blade whirled gently, struck while keeping the beat, cutting choice morsels out of the animal. They fell to the ground as Ling exhaled every time the knife came into contact with the meat and cut it to pieces. 'Hoowha!' he'd say in a low voice.

Zhuang marvelled at so much technique. One evening, he waited for Butcher Ling outside the palace. He saw him from afar, got up from the parapet where he'd been sitting and hailed him. The man stopped, turned around and stared blankly at the young man.

'I am Zhuang Zhou, one of the kitchen supervisors.'

'Glad to hear it, my young friend.'

'I watched you cutting up steers. Tell me, how can you do it with such ease?'

'I have no idea. My knife does the work for me. You know, I've been using the same knife for thirty years, it's not even worn, it's used to it.'

'Explain your method to me.'

'I have no method. I simply see how things work. At first, when I was a young butcher, I used to see the whole steer before me. Three years later, all I saw in the animal were the pieces to be cut out. There on the back, I could recognize the chuck steak in front of the ribs, and the sirloin, the flank steak beneath it, the skirt steak on the belly. I would first cut the animal in my mind before putting a knife into it. Today, the memory of what I've learnt, sight and touch no longer come into play. My blade follows the faults and the splits, spares the veins and tendons and goes around the bones. The pieces separate all by themselves. Satisfied and amused, I wipe my blade and put it back in its scabbard after I've finished my cut.'

'You never feel tired?'

'Why would I feel tired when I'm not making the slightest effort? On the contrary, this labour invigorates me, I don't feel I'm getting older, I'm never sick . . . '

Zhuang marvelled at this lesson. In the long run, however, the experience of a technique was not enough to explain the art of Butcher Ling. In actual fact, he was forgetting the steer and forgetting himself. Zhuang meditated for a long time, back on his parapet again until the sun went down.

CHAPTER FIVE

The Family Goes into Exile

One morning Zhuang was surprised by the commotion as he arrived at the palace. Guards were patrolling all the way to the ramparts. They were nervously searching the wagons that wanted to deliver their wares; they flushed out a band of piglets that scattered over the surrounding streets, took rolls of many-coloured silk out and unrolled them on the ground to make sure no one was hiding inside. Soldiers were running around in front of the monumental gates. They all wore bright red armbands and pushed away the curious who came too close with blows of their garishly painted shields or the shafts of their hooked lances. Zhuang stood at the doorstep of the palace, dumbfounded. An officer recognized him and knowing he was an official in the kitchens, shouted: 'Bring us some wine!' with a gesture ordering him to run down to the basements.

In the staircase, the crush was dangerous. Another officer in a varnished rhinoceros-skin breastplate was bawling out incomprehensible orders. Civil servants of various ranks were going up the stairs with overstuffed sacks over their shoulders, others were going down;

they bumped into each other, yelled and pushed each other, some slipped and were trampled by the others.

'Zhuang! You're here at the right time. Come and help me.'

It was Che, the first scribe. Zhuang asked him what was going on. He knew of course; the scoundrel was always informed before anyone else.

'There was a plot against Duke Wu,' he said, taking his colleague by the sleeve and pushing away the crowd going upstairs with his forearm.

'The plotters were captured?' asked Zhuang, concerned.

'Not at all.'

'So the soldiers are looking for them, right?'

'No, they were cleverly turned and they're part of the plot. Listen . . .' (He stopped on a step despite the chaotic crowd of people going in and out.) 'Duke Wu was strangled with the string of his bonnet.'

'By whom?'

'By Chamberlain Sun.'

'For whom?'

'You're annoying with your eternal questions! For himself, smarty-pants! He took over the throne of Song and now he's hunting down the partisans of Wu-the-Morose. Hurry up, dammit!'

The kitchens were topsy-turvy, poorly lit by the sun that filtered through the small basement windows. The torches were extinguished. A few fires were still burning here and there in the rotisserie. Che was stuffing his hemp sack with whatever he could find—geese, chunks of pork, chicks—and he urged Zhuang to do the same. A spit over there in the back seemed to be turning; you could make out a sizzling shape. Zhuang walked up to it and saw with mute terror that it was not a pig but a man hardly as large as a pig, a dwarf with his face distorted by his last scream. He thought he recognized Song-Ku, his protector, disfigured by cooking. Che swung a well-filled sack over his shoulder:

'Don't waste time!' Che said. 'Let's get out of here—and fast! When order is restored, we have to be far from this mouse trap.'

Che didn't want to go up into the daylight in the flow of this crowd of looters: unnerved soldiers could very well decimate them. Luckily, he was more alert and resourceful than that dreamer Zhuang and he knew all the nooks and crannies of the palace, its hallways, its hidden exits. They took a safer way, away from the mass: a wooden staircase, an almost black corridor, along the arsenals and through a door where all they had to do was push the latch to find themselves in front of the ramparts. They took a deep breath as they leaned against the outside wall. Che noticed his companion didn't have a sack.

'You didn't take anything?'

'Nothing.'

'You silly idiot! It was the perfect time to get some free food.'

'I couldn't manage to do it.'

'Poor Zhuang! The roasted dwarf upset you?'

'Perhaps.'

'You think our new prince will eat him?'

He burst out laughing, then suddenly fell quiet. The alligator-skin drums were beating, the ducal guard must be assembling; it sounded like continuous thunder over the city of Mong. They saw howling soldiers galloping along the rampart walkway. Before one of those little stalls with a flat tile roof passers-by used to relieve themselves, a fat man was struggling with his bare hands against the soldiers who were now surrounding him. Zhuang recognized Prime

Minister Tze-Kao; he was sweating, his triple chin shaking like an empty pouch and in his eyes there was the terror of a hunter thrown to tigers. A soldier thrust his sword into his huge belly, pushed his blade up to the thorax and opened his carcass. Bloody guts poured out of it. Tze-Kao collapsed while other soldiers were pushing his intestines towards the hole of the stall; they fell into the pigsty beneath it.

Che left his sack on the esplanade his family home opened onto; a goose escaped, with ruffled wings. The residence, finely decorated with bellowing, gaudy phoenixes, was in flames. The columns of the door broke apart like half-burnt logs, dragging the uprights of the balconies with them in their fall; the cloth on the windows was on fire, flying around in the hot air. A group of city dwellers were watching the sight without doing anything to put out the inferno.

'What did your father do?' asked Zhuang.

'Minister of War. If the house is burning, my family was executed.'

'You think so?'

'Oh yes, I know so. And who's your father?'

'He's the Superintendent of Gifts and Presents.'

'Not too threatened, then. For the moment, the underlings may be all right, but Sun has fits of madness. He could hide them beneath his bowing and scraping. He managed to federate the ducal guard around him with promises. You've got to watch out for him, he's a fox. The most ravishing concubines of your father's stock won't be enough to temper him, or not for long.'

A cloud of black smoke crowned the fires in this neighbourhood near the palace where the notables lived.

'Let's go see if my house was spared,' Zhuang said, quickening his pace.

Che followed him.

Chou's spacious residence was intact, but when the boys went in, there was motion inside. Wordlessly, soundlessly, silhouettes were hurrying through the galleries and stairways carrying sacks or baskets that they piled up in the courtyard entrance. Zhuang immediately recognized his father from behind; he was putting away the tablets of the ancestors according to their age, with extreme precautions. Che indiscreetly lifted up the lid of a painted wood coffer and discovered a heap of metal coins cut in the shape of a knife. He turned around to Zhuang:

'If your father wants to get out of here, that money will be useless.'

'It's our fortune . . . '

'Yes, in the Song. Elsewhere, that money is worthless.'

'Who's that?' his father said as he discovered the chatterbox.

'He's my colleague, Che. I worked with him in the palace.'

'What's he saying?'

'He says this money will be useless to us.'

'We're leaving for Qi, where I know the king.'

'Over there,' Che went on, 'the coins are cut in the shape of an ant's nose.'

'What do you suggest?' Chou asked helplessly.

'The travelling merchants are putting their goods away and making ready to leave the city for the northeast. Pay them so they accept you in their caravan. If you blend into it, you'll have more chance of not being discovered.'

'You're no dummy, my boy.'

'I'll take care of it,' Che proposed. 'I'll take this money and go see them.'

'Can we trust him?' Chou asked his son.

'Yes, Father, he has to flee, too.'

In the panic, Chou had lost his authority. He sat down on a stool and let them take care of things.

Chou was incapable of reflection, so he rapidly came to his senses. He prudently posted watchmen all around to warn him in case of danger and then distributed the roles. He had decided that since he was the most exposed, he would discreetly leave first, taking with him his ancestors in a clasped casket, his two concubines and Zhuang, his younger son, because unfortunately he'd had a job at the palace. He entrusted to his older son—who felt important—the task of organizing a second departure for the rest of the family and for the dancers of the women's pavilion who could serve as barter. They would leave at night with lanterns to reach their uncle's villa, which was fortified with large clay walls and set in the middle of a park populated with tigers to protect it from brigands.

Che had returned, after distributing the money minted in Song to the merchants. They were in cahoots with them now and Chou hurried to the market square with his few chosen people. Guided by the resourceful Che, they settled down in the midst of the sacks of grain. The convoy left at the start of day. Handcarts merchants with woven hats pushed in front of them, carts drawn by oxen, unstable yokes lugging large reed baskets, tipcarts pulled by clumsy horses . . . The long line of wandering merchants left the city of Mong.

Shaken by the bumps in the road, squeezed between bales of goods, Zhuang didn't feel like he was travelling, carried away into the unknown instead, towards new landscapes, perhaps, that would break his habits. When he looked back, he realized he'd never been afraid in the slightest, despite shrinking from the roasted dwarf who had protected him. 'Oh well! That perfectly roasted piglet joined his ancestors,' he thought afterwards, 'Song-Kou is lucky. However horrible it may be, reality is transient. It's the imagination that's twisting our guts. We think we can guess what's going to happen to us by blackening the situation; we convince ourselves we're in danger, the new duke's soldiers are going to burst in and nail us to the wall with their halberds and burn down the house with their torches. We think in the best-case scenario we'll have to flee, hide and live in permanent fear, but no, there are no soldiers and no danger. When you're not high enough up for people to resent you, you invent roles that build you up—and so put yourself in harm's way. What a counterfeiter the imagination is! We should let things take their course.' Zhuang tried to forget himself by reasoning this way, as Butcher Ling had shown him, so the events had no more hold on him. He had not chosen this attitude, but it preserved him. Zhuang smiled as he fell asleep.

It was a gruelling, interminable voyage. Chou complained about the dried beef the merchants distributed stingily at stopovers. To him, who had given them a large part of his fortune! His two concubines had trouble combing each other's hair. They cursed the discomfort of their cart, where they were treated no better than sacks of grain. Zhuang had put away his brushes and inkstones in a satchel that never left him and during their stops, piqued by curiosity, he would get off to meet his friend Che and talk with the merchants. Southeast of the confluence of the Huai and its tributary, they went through the forest of T'an-Lin. He learnt that it used to be populated by wild-cats, yellow bears, leopards and panthers, but they had disappeared, driven out by the advance of men. Heading northeast, they went by heaps of stones, all that remained of burnt houses, devastated by bandits. They forded streams, rafted across rivers and came across the corpses of travellers who had died of hunger. At last, after the massif of Taishan, they reached the plains of Qi. There, between green hills, Zhuang saw the impressive walls of Linzi, the capital of the kingdom.

CHAPTER SIX

Zhuang Settles in Qi

Qi lived in peace, but it had not always been like that. A few years earlier, by a subtle combination of strategy and diplomacy, this kingdom had backed one neighbour in order to crush another, but the army of a third one had invaded it, reducing its territory and condemning it to peace. This was the Warring States period, unstable, cruel and licentious, when the feudal spirit was giving way to political interests, improbable or ephemeral alliances and betrayals. In three centuries five hundred feudal estates had merged into ten kingdoms jealously guarding their recent power and eager to expand it. Ruse was better than force, there was no promise that could not be broken; efficiency definitively prevailed over nobility of soul, which now seemed ridiculous. Being good and decent was all but forgotten, princes decapitated their enemies by the tens of thousands.

In Qi, commerce was replacing warfare.

It was then an oasis of peace.

When Zhuang entered Linzi, the city had been rebuilt and now overflowed beyond its ramparts. He had never seen such a dense, busy population; Mong, the city he had to flee, resembled a sleepy town by comparison. Here, life never stopped, not even at night; its seven hundred thousand inhabitants were in a state of constant agitation; they swarmed in the workshops, the factories, the stables and the streets, where rows of pavilions a few storeys high were squeezed together. Hurrying carts argued at the crossroads with whiplashes and coarse insults, pedestrians slipped in between the horses when they weren't lingering in bunches before a parade of costumed monkeys or a cockfight organized by showmen taking bets; the copper coins circulated from hand to hand. Wastewater flowed in the middle of the narrow streets and into inner streams full of water lilies straddled by curved bridges. At first, Zhuang was stunned by the noise, for these people didn't talk to each other but howled, and he told himself loud noise was the distinctive feature of imbeciles, since they were unable to master words. Che dragged him through the wild bustle of the crowd to discover a hard-working, insatiable world in which even distractions were taken seriously. They visited tile-covered markets where quantities of silk, cloth, lacquered chairs, shoes, and gutted snakes were sold. The snakes hung by threads and people drank their venom to fortify themselves; in the medicine stalls they found unknown roots and dried sea-horses; next to them, there were over a thousand cages of whistling birds, sides of beef covered with flies people shooed wearily away by waving palm leaves. Elsewhere, pale-green jade mounted into jewels, honey-cakes the merchants steamed on big pots on wheels. They dived into alleyways filled with smoke because the stoves were so close they touched each other, and they ate a soup of reinvigorating peppers in big bowls, as they sat on tiny wicker stools to rest.

The Prime Minister of Qi remembered the hussies Chou had delivered to him to seal a neutrality agreement with Song and he offered him a residence by a stream outside the walls at the Western Gate. This is where Zhuang went back on the evening of his visit to the city. Having left Che at the entrance to an inn and, in a calm place at last, he took out his brushes, picked one, sat down before blank tablets and decided to record his impressions before they escaped. Linzi had terrified him. He couldn't understand the frenzy of those mingled crowds he'd seen struggling all day in their disorderly actions, pursuing a project, a desire—excited, exhausted by their quest. The notables wanted to shine at court, the soldiers sought to distinguish themselves in a feat of arms, the brave aspired to danger, the jurists multiplied the laws, the craftsmen made things from morning to night, the peasants doggedly sowed and planted, the merchants never stopped buying and selling, always more and more, the thinkers wanted their thoughts to follow each other endlessly. They let themselves be carried on by their pursuits, that's what they wanted and that's all they wanted, so they wore themselves out and got lost, they kept running and running, endlessly, but after what? That's what gave them the impression of existing but in no way did they exist.

CHAPTER SEVEN

The Man and the Torrent

Squatting over the skull of a former rival he used as a chamber pot, King Min was meditating on the prosperity of his kingdom of Qi. The richer the country was, the more threatened it was—and rich it was indeed. For how long could Min keep the peace? How long would he be able to preserve it from belligerent, envious princes? Would evil come out of good? The Chinese had the impermanence of things inscribed in their bellies and their heads. They told fables that illustrated this principle. A young man received a magnificent horse as a reward, but he fell and broke both legs while he was galloping; evil came from good, a wound from a reward. War broke out and the princes conscripted young men his age, but he was exempt because he could no longer walk; good came from evil, life came from a wound since all his comrades were massacred. And so on: thus flowed life on, between misleading extremes. King Min let ugly slums prosper in Linzi; brigands from all over found refuge there, but as they didn't commit crimes in the kingdom, he let them rest and prepare their expeditions. Sometimes the army would parade to show its strength without using it; that had been enough up to now.

King Min supported the Mount Hua Association, a creation of his predecessor King Syuan: its purpose was to house itinerant thinkers so they could think in peace and receive a salary. Zhou had intrigued with the Prime Minister so his younger son could belong to this prestigious, lucrative association. Zhuang hesitated, his father pushed him:

'Let me think about it,' said Zhuang.

'Not for too long.'

'Those appointed philosophers wear long square bonnets. Will I have to disguise myself too?'

'You insolent boy! That is not a disguise but a garment. You wear it so everyone can identify your rank!'

'Will I have to recite a doctrine?'

'You'll do whatever you like, or nothing, you'll be paid to dream away and the people of Qi will respect you.'

'A few days more, Father.'

'All right.'

Zhuang took advantage of the respite to roam through the hills, alone now, since his friend Che had disappeared. He sat in the shade of trees and recited the *Book of Odes* or *the Chronicles of the Principality of Lu*. One day, he was disturbed by woodcutters who were clearing a thick forest and hitching the trunks they had cut to the yokes of their water-buffaloes. He got up to let them work, but one of the woodcutters said to him:

'You don't have to leave, mate, we're not gonna' chop down the tree you're sitting under. It's poor wood, good for nothing, no way you can cut it into lumber or even make a fire with it, it smokes too much.'

'You're sparing this tree because it's useless?'

'You got it.'

Zhuang went back home, meditating. He walked unannounced into the ceremonial room of his father who was entertaining himself with his concubines, and, still lost in his thoughts, told him the most significant fact in his morning:

'I saw a tree twisted like a hundred-year-old man. The woodcutters left it alone on the hilltop. They chopped down all the others to turn them into beams or boards. I understood. I, too, *to live out my whole life, I want to be useless.*'

'Just say you want to loaf around.'

'That's right.'

'So, you accept the Mount Hua Association.'

'If they ask nothing of me except wearing that cubical hat . . .'

'They'll only ask you to pretend. You keep a sombre look on your face, you wrinkle your brow, on occasion, you come up with some obscure maxims, you play the inspired thinker. You'll be all the more inspired as no one will understand you, but everyone will look for deep meaning in your words as long as they're vague—that's what counts.'

'That's fine with me, Father.'

'In three days, you will join that worthy institution.'

The next day, Zhuang went wandering around the countryside again. At the end of a long walk, he was attracted by a long, muffled rumbling. He drew near. The noise got louder. At a bend in the pathway the noise grew deafening. It came from an impressive waterfall. The current turned violent as the water flowed over a little wall of flat stones and poured out three hundred feet further down, where white foam seethed and the water vapour formed a light fog. Zhuang was contemplating this landscape and the virulence of nature when he saw, at the edge of this abyss, a man taking off his clothes. With no hesitation, the man dived into the whirling water. Zhuang saw him disappear immediately and said to himself: 'A suicide!' He ran down the path to the edge where the rapid current became more peaceful. He looked for the man who had killed himself so he could fish out his body. He must have been crushed by the force of the whirling water, but no, he saw him a bit further on as he was coming out of the river, shaking his mane. He was singing. Zhuang rushed over to the survivor.

'How did you manage to get out?' asked Zhuang admiringly.

'I swam,' the other answered as he dried himself off in the sun.

'Even a crocodile would have been drowned!'

'I am not a crocodile.'

'What is your secret?'

'I have no secret, my friend. I swim. I follow the whirlpools in the water, I unite with them, I do not reflect on what the right movements might be, I just do them, I am totally in the action. I go up the current when it goes up, I go down when it goes down again.'

'You must have learnt what you're telling me!'

'I was born in these hills, you see, and I grew up in the water, I know its moods and its brutalities, its whims, its bumps and hollows, I never go against it, I become the water that is carrying me, it's my element. If I have mastered the art of swimming, it's not because I wanted to, it's completely natural.'

Zhuang was dazzled by this answer. The swimmer had forgotten he was swimming and that was his talent. Much later, when he composed the major book that bears his name, Zhuang would use this enlightening anecdote, giving the main role to Confucius. He does not describe him as a master who explains everything but as a man anxious to learn. He shows him surrounded by disciples, all parasites with their well-combed chignons, lifting their robes to run towards the hirsute swimmer. And there's Confucius, baffled, questioning this man as if he were only his very humble pupil: 'Confucius was admiring the falls of Lu-Liang. The water fell from a height of three hundred feet and then rushed down foaming over a distance of forty leagues . . .'

CHAPTER EIGHT

Confucius Is an Other

For years, Zhuang remained in his cell of the Mount Hua Association. Its name came from a sacred site of the Chinese West, a steep, gigantic, square rock, part of the smooth straight cliffs that were venerated as a symbol of equality among men. So its adulators, among whom Zhuang found himself by chance and for his own comfort, wore cubical hats to recall the shape of Mount Hua and affirm their spirit of equality. One had to advocate confidence in man, be interested only in others and demand the destruction of all weapons. It was both possible and vain, for Zhuang never saw a trace of the equality they babbled about—still less when servants brought their sustenance to the palace every morning. Zhuang and the servants were absolutely not equal. However, he kept his impressions and feelings to himself, as he had always done; and imitating wisdom didn't bother him, it even amused him, so convinced was he that a man has no calling, any more than a plant, or a bird.

The thousand schools that were proliferating in his time in the midst of wars and pillage all preached with a different voice, and each was certain of being the only one on the right path to saintliness. Discussions and quarrels followed. Doctrines clashed, sages attacked each other in endless, groundless quibbles. They were calling for universal peace in a terribly violent way.

Zhuang learnt to distinguish the principal schools by their outward signs. Those who demanded a return to nature dressed in goatskins and ate acorns, they wore clogs or straw slippers and had big calves from working day and night to fulfil the dream of their master, Mozi. That master was so interested in productivity that he cited as an example the mythical Yao the Great who dug canals connecting the Blue River to the Yellow River, irrigated the land and diverted floods. Mozi wanted to save a world in disarray through toil, but for peace and love to triumph, he forbade music and ritual. One should no longer weep for the dead, nor empty a gourd of wine and laugh loudly, nor dance or rejoice. These sad Mozists were subdivided into many factions which called each other heretics. They clashed and jeered at each other in the name of the public good. Others scorned knowledge, expressed no opinion for fear of being prejudiced and contented themselves with a narrow present, comparing themselves to a stump that does not need wisdom to be in conformity with the law of species and things. Still others explained that the ancients had understood everything, so it was better to remain mute and empty: 'Be vague and inexistent, calm as a body of pure water.'

You could recognize the Confucianists by their round bonnets, their clodhoppers with square toes and the profusion of charms hanging from their belts—amulets to attract success, long life or abundant crops. They had dried out Confucius' teaching. Generations of disciples had stiffened the Master's witticisms, stripped him of the slightest humour, washed him, reduced him to sonorous precepts which had some worth in his chaotic time but had now turned into a doctrine. Confucius was right to mistrust followers, too eager, too smug, too sure of themselves. Yet he said wisdom was transmitted not by words but by experience. Today all that remained was words, tirelessly repeated. And yes, he defended a kindly, just upbringing and hoped to compel men to be polite, kind and obedient . . .

The scholar Wen Tse shared Zhuang's cell and made fun of the elite schools:

'You can canalize a river,' he would say, 'But not make it flow back to its source. This degenerate world is swarming with thinkers. Like brigands, they're not the critique of the world but its products!'

'If they're useless, so much the better,' Zhuang would say.

'Useless? That would be fine. They're harmful. Their saintliness smells rancid, even if people dote on it. They're blind! Deaf! Let's get rid of saintliness, let's eradicate wisdom, yes, let's be wary of those entrepreneurs in goodness!'

Zhuang was shaken by his companion's strong words, but in his heart he agreed. Wen Tse, nicknamed The Ugly, had one leg shorter than the other, he limped low and had no nose ever since soldiers surprised him pilfering and sliced it off with their sword. At first, people only gave him a sidelong glance, for he made them uneasy, but then you got used to his battered mug and deformed gait, and as soon as he talked, you could even find him handsome:

'You see, Zhuang, Confucius simply wanted words to have a meaning everyone could understand, in the South as well as in the West. He thought the object of speech was to be understood, not to jabber on about nothing! Caught between the loutish jokes of the commoners and the ponderousness of the schools, we truly lack lightness!'

Wen Tse would launch into a little dance step, grotesque but light. He flapped his arms like wings, his feet lame like the feet of an albatross, but suddenly, carried along by his gestures, he was no longer deformed.

One day, Wen Tse and Zhuang learnt that Mencius was coming to live in Linzi, invited by King Min in person, who adulated him. Mencius was the only thinker who claimed to prolong Confucius' teaching, which he had simplified into a dogma. It was his mission, he would say pompously. Extremely honoured by his arrival, King Min had put the Jixia Academy at his disposal. It was at the gates of the city and under a hill, a vast hall lined with apartments for him and his best disciples; the others had to find lodgings in nearby hamlets or at the inns in the neighbourhood of ill repute, which enabled them to put their saintliness to the test among the pickpockets, beggars and future highway robbers. Mencius liked order and hierarchy. He also liked honours and acted servile before the princes to whom he owed his renown. It was for them alone he spoke, even as he feigned compassion for the common people, whom he despised: people with no manners, barbarians, idiots. Zhuang saw Mencius cross the city with great pomp, clothed in a gilded tunic, waving a fan in a nonchalant way that was meant to be noble, astride a horse going at a walk, followed by his troupe of four hundred disciples chanting the *Book of Odes*. People crowded in front of the houses and at the windows to watch the braggart go by; the spectacle was enough to distract them momentarily from the usual street performers, jugglers with lighted torches, or trainers of performing monkeys.

Mencius was haughty and impassive, but delighted with King Min's welcome. One could tell from the contented smile he was incapable of hiding. He liked to think he was a moral authority and indeed he was, when crowds of the faithful came to listen to him in the courtyard of his new abode. He claimed men were good at birth and problems only arose from bad governments, but he knew how to turn his brilliant phrases in such a way that they flattered the mighty; besides, he would add, the princes I associate with are models of virtue since they rule the world through filial piety. This served him as a refrain:

'What are rituals,' he would say, 'If not the manifestation of respect? Nothing more. When the fathers are respected, the sons rejoice. When an intelligent man has neither master nor standards, he invariably becomes a thief. If he's courageous, he inevitably becomes a brigand and if he's competent, he never fails to stir up trouble . . .'

Then he would inveigh against his adversaries—something Confucius never did—to the delight of his enraptured disciples:

'What does that madman Hsun Tzu say? He says, he dares to say, that even Emperor Yao had a penchant for savagery! That men are possessed by the lure of gain from the minute they are born! And by the way, what does he think of the constraints of education? Nothing. He forgets to talk about that!'

'What a joker,' Wen Tse the Ugly said to Zhuang.

Thanks to their cubical bonnets they had been admitted to listen to the Master.

'I've had it,' said Wen Tse, grabbing his friend's arm and pushing him towards the courtyard gate. 'Come on, let's go, let that two-faced clown speechify before his assembly, come on, let's go . . .'

'He annoys you that much?'

'He doesn't annoy me, he exasperates me.'

As they were going back to the lodgings of the Mount Hua Association, Wen Tse explained:

'He doesn't just betray or reduce Confucius, but everything he says is a fabrication. He wants to advise rich princes and take advantage of their largesse. They never listen to him. He knows it and couldn't care less because they're flattered by his presence, as they would be by a beautiful courtesan. Mencius is living on his reputation, he's surrounded by a bunch of simpletons who glorify him as soon as he opens his mouth.'

'You know him well?'

'Oh yes, I know where he comes from.'

'Where does he come from?'

'He's a chameleon and always has been: he takes on the colour of the stand on which he's put. He was jealously raised by his mother—cosseted, really—so concerned she was about his future! She watched over him closely and had to move three times for his sake. At first they lived next to a slaughterhouse, but young Mencius spent his time imitating the cries of the animals they were slaughtering. So his mother took him to a lodging near a market. What did he do? He played the merchant. That kid was like a sponge! Then, he and his mother moved near a school; he became studious from one day to the next. Since he had a pronounced taste for bossing people around, he went into teaching.'

To see how far Mencius had departed from Confucius, Zhuang studied the life of the Master closely. He went back to the *Analects*—the sayings collected by his disciples—and read them with great attention. At first, he found numerous precepts and details emphasized by Mencius on filial piety and the necessity of order. In many passages, Confucius appeared to be fussy about ritual and held the firm opinion that the old hemp bonnet be replaced by a bonnet of silk, or how to bow with folded hands at the bottom of the stairs rather than at the top. Nonetheless, he found real pearls there, far removed from the conformism Confucius was confined to. His first pupils noted: 'The Master had freed himself from four things; he had no preconceived ideas, no inflexible positions, no dogmatic certainty and no egocentrism.' It was the exact opposite of Mencius and his mad race for honours.

How had Confucius lived? What was his life like? He was unsightly, hunchbacked and had a frightful toad-like head with thick lips. He was a schoolmaster, disillusioned by his students. He was unstable: a vegetarian but for three months only, married at nineteen but divorced at twenty-three because his wife couldn't cook. He taught history, poetry and property, and often talked about the good emperors of yesteryear, Yao and Shun, always erasing their faults, and saying nothing about the way they massacred the little kings who bothered them.

Confucius rubbed shoulders with the powerful but with a teacher's manners and not, like Mencius, to get rich. After a happy try at advising a prince in the state of Lu, he was swept away by intrigues and sent off. He was fifty years old. Driven away as he was, he wandered for thirteen years. With a handful of faithful followers of whom he was not particularly fond, he went through the provinces to spread the word, an obvious word no one wanted to hear. Undesirable everywhere, he no longer knew where his place was. Here, calumny pushed him out. There, in a village in the state of Wei, he was almost torn to pieces because he was the spitting image of Yang-the-Tiger, a wicked adventurer feared by the villagers. He went through wars and uprisings, ran into bandits and knew famine. He only acquired his fame when he died, he who kept repeating 'The bird chooses the tree but the tree does not choose the bird.' They built a mausoleum for him against his will and he crossed the centuries misrepresented as a supreme educator.

If Zhuang came back today, he would be horrified: Confucius, the homeless scholar who only travelled to learn freely and immerse himself in the world, who bore hardship and insults, was now the embodiment of restrictive morality. His influence—utterly corrupted—spread all over Asia, overflowed the borders of China, took root in Korea and Japan. In Hanoi, where his thought entered through the wagons of an invading army, they betrayed Confucius as much as they listened to him. In the Temple of Literature, which the French colonizers called the crow pagoda because of the birds that landed in flocks on the mango trees at the entrance, there, amidst courtyards too square, lawns too closely mowed, pools too clear, hedges too trimmed, his gigantic, bright red effigy sat enthroned in the half-light of a colonnaded temple. Visitors contemplated him from behind a balustrade. Around the perimeter of the Court of the Sages, shops offered, between the postcards, key-rings in white plastic imitating ivory with the words *longevity, success, perseverance* inscribed on them in Chinese characters. Schoolchildren in uniforms lined up to beg for good grades on their exams. Among the books displayed there were manuals of wisdom in simplistic formulas and a stack of Bill Gates' memoirs. Zhuang would not have recognized his Confucius; he would have craved for brushwood, surprises, whimsy, disorder, laughter.

CHAPTER NINE

Towards War

When Zhuang turned twenty, his father visited him at the Mount Hua Association, an unusual occurrence, since he let his son live his own life. Zhuang was sitting under a banyan tree furrowed with exposed and complicated roots. A spot where he often talked with his friend Wen Tse.

'Come to the palace with me,' Chou said. 'The refugees from Song have been asked to give their opinion.'

'Father, I have no opinion about anything.'

'Your son is on the road to holiness,' Wen Tse chimed in, with a touch of irony.

'Holy or not, he must go with me,' Chou insisted. 'A clandestine delegation from Song has just arrived to persuade King Min to drive out the usurper who drove us out!'

'Chamberlain Sun?'

'Duke Sun! In a few years, he so brilliantly succeeded in getting himself detested that they call him Sun-the-Evil-One in the country.'

'Why, Father?'

'That's what we're going to find out. Come!'

'I'll follow you,' Wen Tse said.

A mess of palanquins and carriages were parked on the esplanade in front of Min's over-ornate palace. The coachmen told them the notables from Song were already in the audience hall. Chou, his son, and Wen Tse made their way inside and stood discreetly in the last row. They heard the loud voice of Baron Qiu-Chu sound out before the throne. He had tucked his peacock-plumed helmet under his arm and was forcefully informing the king and his court about the situation in Song with an abundance of details.

'My lord, Sun's main wife could not bear child, despite her repeated attempts. The soothsayers and magicians were unable to solve her problem, so she came up with a subterfuge behind Sun's back. Pretexting invocations to the good genies of fertility, she had surrounded herself with grimacing statues and tried to have a child with just about anybody. She retired to her private rooms and forbade entry, even to the Duke of Song. He accepted this whim, attributing it to her sorrow at not being able to give birth. Meanwhile, procurers chose fiery young fellows for her in the brothels of the city and brought them in every morning in curtained carriages, disguised as courtesans. They took off their female attire in a poorly lit antechamber and, naked as a worm, waited their turn. That could last all day. Although they were sustained by unguents and witches' brews, the unfortunate youths were left exhausted. These incessant visits did not remain discreet for long, so loud were the groans and cries of the duchess that they could be heard up to the duke's bedroom. This carnal play, so popular and natural in our lands, which strengthens the yin of men and the yang of women in beneficial harmony, became a tiresome labour for dozens of young men. Secret at first, these liaisons were soon common knowledge; coachmen even joked about it in their drives across town.

'Amusing,' said King Min. 'And then what?'

'Well, the Duke of Sun's first favourite quickly replaced his first wife. That's when our troubles began . . .'

Baron Qiu-Chu sighed; he mopped his brow with a scarf and continued his story. He told him who this concubine was: a young intriguer with a sweet voice but feline nails. From then on, she replaced the official wife at court, in bed and in Duke Sun's heart. She rapidly took on disproportionate importance through her demands and whims. She had the beauty of those golden-brown Barbarians in the West and the Duke obeyed her like a trained monkey. She dominated him. So now everyone in Song took care of their own business and neglected the public good. The country sunk because it was no longer governed. When the sovereign does not set the example, everything falls apart.

'One extravagance among a hundred others, O Mighty Lord,' the baron continued. 'The concubine got bored so Sun tried to entertain her. She loved to hear the sound of silk when it's ripped: it gave her a sensual pleasure that made her shudder and groan. The duke had quantities of silk pieces ripped up for her . . .'

'Excellent for the silk mills of Song,' King Min said.

'Not at all, My Lord, for Duke Sun never paid. He said it was a tribute, so that his new mistress could smile again. And there's worse. To amuse her one evening, the duke had the alarm fires ignited to simulate an attack by the voracious kingdoms of the West. His barons immediately raised armies, distributed cuirasses and lances to the peasants who were busy ploughing the land; they ran to Mong and realized the mockery when the concubine burst out laughing at their downcast faces. We may wager that the next time there's an alert, no one will mobilize to save the throne. The fires will be useless. The time has come, o noble Min, to undertake a punitive invasion of the kingdom of Song.'

'To put you onto the throne, Qiu-Chu?'

'I would be your ally, o mighty Lord, at the borders of Wei and Qin.'

'I'll think about it.'

'I think the time has come . . .'

As soon as the audience was adjourned and the king had retired, Chou came over to the baron, who recognized him.

'Chou, you old rascal!'

'Rascal yourself! Tell me, isn't the first wife of Sun-the-Evil-One your daughter?'

'Yes, as you well know.'

'Don't you want to avenge her for Sun's indifference?'

'He's no longer fit to rule.'

'Ever since your daughter no longer has his favours? And you don't either?'

'Probably.'

'What happened to my family? I haven't heard about them for years.'

'Because you didn't try. Your elder son did not escape as you expected. He stayed in Mong and took over your troupe of dancers and courtesans for himself.'

'He supplied Sun?'

'Exactly. His favourite comes from him—or rather, from you.'

'If the duke falls, he falls, too?'

'Exactly.'

'Too bad for him! He betrayed his father.'

'Which one of you betrayed the other more?'

King Min was pondering. Was he going to start a war? Qi's army had been just for show for so long, with a permanent cadre of officers in charge of recruiting the peasants they needed, but they were rusty from inaction. Wanting to hear some advice, good or bad, before deciding, the king summoned wise men around him, among them Wen Tse, whose reputation for being outspoken had spread beyond the walls of the peaceful Association of Mount Hua. Wen had asked his young friend Zhuang to assist him so as not to lose a word of the deliberations—all that just to instruct him.

'I know,' the king said to Wen Tse, 'that as a matter of principle, you want to throw all weapons in the trash . . .

'Great King, principles can evolve as situations change.'

'Tell me if I have the capacity to fight battles against Song. People in those hills are said to be short-sighted slugs.'

'Not all of them, My Lord. My friend Zhuang here comes precisely from that region and his stupidity has yet to be demonstrated. Ask yourself instead whether you can arm a hundred thousand men.'

'How can I recruit so many soldiers? Many have only known peace.'

'You must make wise use of punishments and rewards to stir such a mass.'

'The punishments for thieves and traitors are so horrible they're only used now to scare them. They've never been used.'

'You must be sure they are effective.'

'How?'

'Simple! Have the stables of your palace set on fire. We'll see if your subjects come running with buckets filled with water!'

King Min was convinced by Wen Tse's words and gave orders for the fire to be lit. The inhabitants of the capital, too busy at their jobs, did not lift a finger to stop the disaster, although many came to admire the blaze and listen to the whinnying of the horses stamping among the flames. Wen Tse gave a last piece of advice to the king:

'Mighty Lord, now go post a royal proclamation in the city. You will say that the families of the brave men who died putting out the fire will receive a lifelong pension and so will they if they survive. Threaten those who refuse to fight the fire, tell them they'll be found and plunged into boiling water to cook until dead.'

And thus it was done. Immediately, thousands of volunteers, lured by the promise of a pension and the fear of boiling water rushed to the area around the palace. They had smeared themselves with mud and their clothes were wet to escape the fire. They managed to put it out before it could gnaw at the walls of the palace. The next day, King Min asked his generals to raise an army of a hundred thousand men.

'The king was right,' Zhuang said to his companion. 'What's the use of principles?'

'What do we say, at the academy? Weapons are disastrous. That was Master Wu's point of view and our king has studied his treaty on strategy. I subscribe to it. I remain faithful to our principle.'

'You could have tried to dissuade King Min from starting a war . . .'

'What's the use of a lute player's talent at the court of a prince who prefers the sound of drums? What does Min want? He knows Song is fertile and he really wants to establish himself there. The big always eats the small, but that's not enough. Song will allow him to approach, get around, and spy on its big rivals, Wei and Qin, as that's where the threat will come from one day.'

'On a bad pretext!'

'On an excellent pretext. He wants to overthrow Duke Sun, who is detested by his people and who suffer because of him. War is the art of lying nowadays, the king thinks it may be enough to display his force so as not to use it, and become a righter of wrongs.'

'But still, a war!' Zhuang lamented.

'Listen to our great old sages,' said Wen Tse, 'Listen to what Grand Marshal T'sien said: 'If you must attack a State to show your love of humanity, you must not hesitate to attack; if you must use arms to silence arms, you should not hesitate to use your sword.'

'And old Lao said, 'Every victory is celebrated with funeral rites.''

King Min's army was ready by the dry season. It made a ceremonious departure from the city of Linzi to intervene in Song. Disguised as soldiers, those peasants who had traded their spades for lances and their straw coats for sewn leather armours were formidable to behold. They all possessed a plot of land and paid the grain tax; they did not leave for the war gaily, but their officers terrified them and discipline bound them together. They advanced by brigades, almost by villages, behind the oriflammes dancing in the wind, displaying the Red Bird or the White Tiger. Next came the war chariots, drawn by well-fed, fat, thick-necked horses wearing little bells in their bits. Following them in the narrow boxes set on two-wheel chariots stood the drivers, flanked by a lancer and an archer with three arrows stuck in his armband. Then the crossbowmen with polished ox-skin knee-guards; after them, the halberdiers, many with bear-tooth collars and brightly coloured shields tied to their forearms raised high. Then, the horsemen wearing tunics and pants like the nomads of the North from the Mongol plains where the strong winds raised sandstorms. Behind them panthers and bears trained to attack: their cages would be opened before the enemy; finally, the catapults and the towers on wheels, preceding a thousand wagons with leather caissons filled with supplies.

'Those killing machines make my blood run cold,' Zhuang said.

'Fear alone drives them forward,' Wen Tse said, 'Otherwise they'd run back home at full speed.'

CHAPTER TEN

The Return Home

Zhuang chose to go back to Song with his father and the delegation led by Baron Qiu-Chu. They would follow King Min's army from a distance. Min was to put them in power once the usurper was swept away. Zhuang bid farewell to his friend Wen Tse, who had no reason whatsoever to accompany him and many to stay in Linzi:

'Life changes wherever you are. Do I need to wear out my shoes day after day to understand the world? Oh, no! Travelling is tiring. Even if this war is brief, it will break both our countries, ruins are as pretty here as they are elsewhere. Tell me, what do I need? A few jars of wine and a tree trunk to lean my back against.'

'I enjoyed our conversations . . .

'Well, forget them! The passing of time has already erased our words and our joyful moments. You're twenty, I'm not.'

They got drunk one last time. And then Zhuang joined the convoy as it left, leaving Wen Tse snoring on the grass. Lying in a wagon full of cushions and blankets, rocked by the regular grinding of the wheels, he stayed drunk for three whole days. He could hardly recall the faces of Xing and Ching, the very young courtesans his father had offered him to keep him tenderly occupied.

There were many stops; in the evening, servants set up the large whitewashed felt tents and lit braziers to keep away pests. They finally arrived in Song and were shocked by the panorama they discovered. Just wars were not clean wars. King Min's generals methodically sacked the regions they went through: their soldiers were paid by the number of heads they cut off and they put their hearts into the task. In a plain where sated vultures circled overhead, they estimated there were several thousand headless corpses bathing in black blood, congealed like a cold sauce. Holding his nose with a scarf to filter the acrid stench of the dead bodies, Zhuang picked up the blade of a halberd with these words engraved on it: 'To the left of the big steep hill.' It was the address of the foundry the weapon came from.

CHAPTER ELEVEN

In the Mulberry Forest

The land of Song began to live again, but differently. There were soldiers everywhere, even in the fields that had to be cleaned by burning heaps of decomposed bodies at gigantic stakes. The thick smoke of these furnaces could be seen from the borders. Sun-the-Evil-One, his hated concubine and his faithful followers had been massacred and hanged by the feet from the beams of the palace for the edification of the people—among them Zhuang's older brother, abandoned to green flies. Gone was his chance to ever show off at the altar of the ancestors; besides, his father decided he had never existed and destroyed all his birth documents. Since his second brother, a dull boy, had died in an epidemic, Zhuang found himself in the official role of the elder, but he refused its servitudes. Filial piety was becoming an adulterated notion. He had learnt in Qi to neglect most of the rites and his father was busy starting a new family with his latest favourites. The times were troubled, fortunes were changing hands, licentiousness was widespread and everyone took advantage of it.

King Min had established a protectorate in Song; he entrusted its fate to the puppet Baron Qiu-Chu, who was now sitting on the throne. To assist him, Baron Chu called rebels and exiles to support him. Thus Chou regained his former prerogatives. He easily reconstituted his network of dancers and nimble girls who'd been wrenched from the confines of the Chinese West by caravanners. Influential once again, he thought of promoting his heir. The very notion of holding a position was abhorrent to Zhuang but he remembered his friend Wen Tse's wise maxim: 'Prudence is a force, not a virtue,' and he prudently bowed to his father's will so nobody would bother him.

Zhuang was appointed Supervisor of Lacquers.

Lacquer played an important role in the economy of Chinese kingdoms. It was painted on makeup boxes, dishes and bamboo furniture. It came from a native tree that had to be bled for the sap to flow into small buckets attached to the trunks. The lacquerers retrieved that natural gum, then filtered and heated it. After clarification, it was applied to thin wooden plaques and dried in humid air. Zhuang's role was to make sure these meticulous operations were properly carried out. He held a long rod tied to his wrist with which he was to rub the backs of the insolent and the lazy, but he refused to use it and preferred to encourage the workers through words and example. He was personally in charge of the black lacquer, spreading the gum on a cold surface that he coloured with charcoal smoke.

Zhuang was entitled to private accommodations. He differentiated himself from the other civil servants who settled comfortably into massive residences because he only requested a modest house of wood and clay, with an untrimmed thatched roof where colocynth grew freely. He had picked it on a hillock at the edge of the Mulberry Forest. He felt closer to the peasants and to his workers there, even if he did have silk covers on his rush mat. In the evening, he stood at his door and watched the men growing millet in their small plots and the women in short clothes made of animal skins weaving hemp or braiding nettles. Zhuang grew a few acres of vegetables on the eastern slopes, but as he was busy watching over the Garden of Lacquers every day, he left Xing and Ching, whom he had brought with him, to gather vegetables and cook meals, which they usually ate in front of their house. Then they would drink rice wine and play the lute; their music sounded far into the countryside. At the hour the birds grew still, they went back inside to bed by lantern light and sank together into sleep and dreams. Zhuang's life flowed on in perfect monotony.

When spring returned, Zhuang and his concubines would get up before dawn to enjoy the first sun warming the waters of the stream. The ducks had come back and they watched them swimming between the willows on the bank; the girls would then run in to bathe and splash in the water. The plum trees were already in full bloom and soft green grass was taking over the burnt fields of winter. One morning, as he arrived at the Garden of Lacquers, Zhuang noticed a child squatting and beating the bank with a switch.

'What are you doing?'

'I'm driving away the crabs, Mister Supervisor. It's their season, they're coming back.'

'Leave them alone.'

'Foreman Tien Wei ordered me to do it . . .'

'Listen carefully, my boy. T'ien Wei is an idiot! He falls for every superstition without ever using his brain! He says ashes engender flies and magpie droppings poison hedgehogs! He has no idea! He never saw that! He repeats nonsense and spreads it all over! Crabs stop lacquer from drying? Of course, if they skip about on it with their legs! But lacquer dries under canopies protected by fences, you know they do. Crushing crabs near the stream is useless.'

'I know, Mister Supervisor.'

'And you're obeying a senseless order!'

'What else can I do, Sir?'

'You're right. You're obeying. You must obey. It will always be like that. You don't have the means to rebel. I know. Make T'ien Wei happy. Do whatever you want.'

'I don't want anything, Sir. I do what I'm ordered to do and I can't argue.'

'Yes,' Zhuang said thoughtfully, 'Yes, but your freshwater crabs, those soft crabs you're so stupidly killing, you could put them into a bag and bring them to me. I'll cook them. Have you ever tasted any?'

'No, Sir.'

'When they're steamed, they turn red, they're excellent. You'll eat them with me. OK?'

'Yes, Mister Supervisor.'

As he chatted with the boy, Zhuang saw a cortege of palanquins coming out of the city and moving towards the vermillion arch of the wooden bridge. The first wife of the new duke opened her curtain and put a foot on the ground, the second wives imitated her, and so did the rest of them, all in green tunics to celebrate the return of the springtime, its sweetness and golden light. They were carrying baskets and went into the forest to pick mulberry leaves. Zhuang and the boy approached the visitors.

'Ah, it's our Supervisor,' the first wife said.

'Are you here to welcome the spring?' Zhuang asked, taking off his cap.

'We've come to encourage the cultivation of silkworms by setting an example.'

'What example?'

'It's our role,' the first wife said without answering the question.

Zhuang was going to say that to set an example, you had to spin or weave, but a group of people came out of the forest at the same moment. A bald man introduced himself as a craftsman and said he wanted to give something of his art to the first wife of his master Qiu-Chu. He extended his arms towards her, opened his fists with his palms turned upward and everyone could see two identical mulberry leaves in his hands. Even from very close up, they had the same nervures, the same colour, the same delicacy, and yet, while one had just been ripped off a branch, the other was chiselled out of ivory. You could not tell them apart. The craftsman was happy with them. He explained that it had taken him three years to imitate a mulberry leaf. The ladies gathered around him and marvelled at his work. Zhuang said nothing and went back to his house. He took the little boy by the hand and grumbled:

'He lost three years of his life imitating a leaf! The sky and the earth don't need three years: a breath of air is enough! Perfection only exists in nature. When you imitate nature, you always do less well. People want to domesticate it, correct it, mutilate it! Nature will take its revenge. Air and water will transport poisons!'

As they walked, Zhuang explained to the boy that Mo Ti had built a flying machine and Pan Chu, wooden horses that drew carts; Ning Che had invented a wooden and leather automaton that sang when you touched its chin.

'I prefer the flight of the kite, the horse and the voice. Be careful not to let the artificial destroy the natural.'

'Yes, Sir.'

'People become crazy in cities! They build cages for birds and think they have a singer at home. If you want to hear the chatting of birds, my boy, it's better to plant a tree.'

'Yes, Sir'

'By the way, what's your name?'

'I don't have a name.'

'Even when your family calls you?'

'They call me Number Six because I'm the sixth son.'

They arrived at the house, where Xing and Ching were heating up water in a cauldron. They had just come out of the river and were drying off by moving in the sun.

'The water's already hot? Perfect,' Zhuang said, as he gave Ching the bag where the crabs were still swarming around. 'Xing! Go get the steamer to cook these little creatures!'

The child was captivated by the two women, by their long, sleek black hair, long enough to clothe them, for all they wore were their flashy jewels, like the wild girls they once had been. The boy stood transfixed watching them, their smiles and their velvety skin; Zhuang pictured himself back when he was living in the women's quarters at the north end of the big family home. While the crabs were steaming and changing colour, he couldn't help telling the kid the thoughts that had been stirring in him for some time: he told him that the strength of Xing and Ching came from their instinct, which guided them far better than any artificial intentions.

They ate the crabs, burning their fingers. Their shells were so tender there was no need to break them apart.

The next evening, Number Six returned with a new bag of crabs, less dazzled by Zhuang's weighty sayings than by how free and spontaneous his concubines were.

'Tell me, my boy, won't your father worry if you walk up to my place every day?'

'No, Mister Supervisor. And why would he worry? I don't exist.'

The Supreme Director of Lacquers paid a visit to Zhuang one morning. He stepped out of his horse-drawn carriage on a folding stepladder and found the Supervisor dancing in front of his eastern door.

'Oh!' he said, 'You're doing exercises to improve your flexibility?'

'I'm learning to fly.'

'You joker! Even if you had wings, you'd be too heavy!'

'I still need to study the mystery of the winds that carry real birds.'

The Supreme Director smiled at this eccentricity but was truly surprised to see Zhuang's house, far too rustic for him:

'You have no lacquered table? No chair, no bowl, no goblet? Your position gives you the right to own furniture and dishes from our own workshops, you know that, don't you?'

'Yes, but to eat I have my hands, to drink I have calabashes of wine a peddler brings me on his mule. To water my vegetable garden, I have the dew or water from the river that I carry up on my back. Sometimes I shoot a pheasant with my crossbow. There are so many fish in the river I can take my pick.'

He pointed to the spot where Xing and Ching were fishing with a net and then they walked down together towards the meadows. Chatting about the quality of lacquers, they stopped before a well. Five strapping men, naked to the waist and covered in sweat, were going down into the well to fill up their big earthenware jars. They climbed back up, bending under the weight of their jars before they watered their pumpkins. The Supreme Director considered this absurd activity and called over one of the peasants:

'To draw water effortlessly, there are machines, my good man. I'll teach you how to build a seesaw pump and you'll be able to draw water without tiring yourself out.'

'A machine?' one of the peasants said, curling his lip. 'I don't want to set a bad example.'

'How's that?'

'The man who invents skilful mechanisms becomes the victim of his own invention. We know how to make your pump but we don't want it.'

'Morons!' the Supreme Director said as he resumed his walk.

'They're right,' Zhuang said as they walked away from the well and its human waterwheel.

'But really! With machines, the peasants will produce more, make more money, and they'll have an easier life . . .'

'That's just it, Noble Director. They sense that we quickly become the slaves of objects. What would happen with the effects of your machine? They'll want to make more and more money, they'll produce too much and one day the machines will replace them. Then profiteers and thieves will step in. They're refusing to be devoured, that's all. They are wise.'

'Wise or mad? Come, come, Mister Supervisor, what words!'

'I'm just showing you a possible chain of events.'

'You're not a man of your time, Mister Supervisor! I could tell when I inspected your cottage. You certainly do your work to per-fection, and I have nothing against you except for your false ideas.'

'My ideas are false, Supreme Director, Sir, because they are not your ideas. Are you so sure of them?'

'Of course!'

As Zhuang had no desire to spend his time persuading anyone, he fell quiet. But the Director wanted him to change his mind and embarked on a series of explanations:

'If you were asked to return to the time when men lived naked in caves, when women were no more than females, when rivers could only be crossed by swimming and mountains on foot, when men planted their teeth into the bloody meat of freshly killed animals before they had the idea of cooking them, what kind of song would you sing then? Our princes civilized us, and during the time of Yao the Great, craftsman Chouei invented the compass, the T-square and the first ploughs!'

'Chouei is an exemplary character who never existed.'

'But the plough exists, and thanks to the compass and the set square we've built bridges, roads, boats, houses and, to feed ourselves, we've farmed meadows that used to lie fallow.'

Zhuang answered:

'When holy men wanted to establish justice and rites, people obeyed them at first, and after that they tore each other apart. The holy men destroyed their spontaneity, that's what I mean to say. And then they wanted to accumulate goods, honours and power.'

'Do you think so?' the Director replied. 'Murder and plunder are natural instincts. All the princes of yesteryear did was to rein in our impulses to seek harmony.'

'Harmony through constraint? A pretty business! Look at horses living in the state of nature. Putting a bit in their mouths and a saddle on their backs, penning them up in stables and taming them with a whip was enough to turn them into sly and vicious animals.'

The Supreme Director sighed:

'My poor friend, you're dreaming of an ideal land!'

'You said it, I'm dreaming. All men sleep for a third of their lives, all men dream.'

'But you, you never stop dreaming.'

They left each other, neither convinced by the opposing argument. The Supreme Director climbed back into his carriage. From that time on, Zhuang wrote down his nightly dreams on tablets.

CHAPTER TWELVE

The Monkey Farm

Master Houei arrived in Song on a short horse that did not exist in the region. His legs almost reached the ground and he wore a flat-brimmed hat. A servant was pulling a mule along by the bridle, overloaded with bundles, while another held a yellow parasol over the horseman. Zhuang was lying in the shade of a gnarled almond tree when he saw this crew trotting on the road to Mong.

'Hey! Traveller! Where are you coming from with your load?'

'From Wei,' the other answered, stopping his white horse.

The servant with the parasol helped him alight, that is, given the short height of the steed, he swung his left leg over its neck. Zhuang got up, swishing his horn fan:

'So what are you hoping to find here that is lacking in the great kingdom of Wei?'

'I hope people in Song have a better ear.'

'They're deaf in Wei?'

'Deaf as a post. They prefer the clanking of swords. I am Master Houei and I teach music.'

He stroked a water-buffalo-hide case tied to his mule, which most probably contained a cithara.

'A fine profession,' Zhuang said, 'I play the lute. Will you help me improve?'

'Sure, if they employ me at the court.'

'Ask for Chou. He's the one who supplies the palace with dancing girls and musicians.'

'Should I say you sent me?'

'He's my father. You'll tell him you met the Supervisor of Lacquers drowsing under a tree.'

'I will improvise a piece from our repertoire for him and he'll understand me better than with words.'

'Music has strict rules, too . . .'

'Maybe so, but anyone can be touched by the notes of my cithara, all over China, in every kingdom, in shacks, in palaces. People don't need to know how to play to understand, whereas with words it's quite different. Look at merchants. They're illiterate and hang up signs with pictures on them over their shops, a wooden fish here, a hunk of coal there, a mug of wine cut from a board, ox horns. Above all, they sing about their products in the language of the streets. They're the echo of the people, of the working class, with their rhyming melodies and the cries of the strolling peddlers. That's why in Wei there is an Office of Ballad Supervision; policemen take note of the words of the fishmonger or the coal seller to record the mood of the Prince's subjects—what is making them happy or discontented. They dive into the hellish world of opinions expressed through these songs . . .'

As the two tired valets hoisted Master Houei on his little horse again, he asked:

'Is the city far? We're worn out by our long trip.'

'Mong is quite near. Once you go over that hill, you'll see the ramparts.'

A few days later, Zhuang buttoned up his least worn-out black tunic; he was to go to town to accompany a delivery of lacquered armchairs ordered by the palace. On the way, one of the wooden wheels of his cart split over a rut. He and his lacquerers tried to repair it with rope and somehow they managed to drag it to the shop of a wheelwright's at the gates of Mong. The man who greeted them had white hair gathered in a bun and the ravaged face of a centenarian. As he was alone, Zhuang called out:

'Tell me, can you or your son repair that wheel for me?'

Without a word, the man looked closely at the defective wheel, felt around it and delivered his verdict:

'Can't repair that. It'll probably break again.'

'Do you have spare wheels?'

'No, I make 'em to measure.'

'Will it take long?'

'Half a day.'

Zhuang asked his master lacquerer to run to the palace and bring back a wagon to make the delivery. Then he sat down on a big stone while the wheelwright was picking out his wood. Zhuang watched him work. The man cut the wood, bent and adjusted it without calculating anything, using the awl or the hammer with smooth, precise gestures. He neither rushed nor dawdled. The wood seemed to obey him. His wheel was taking on a perfectly round shape. As soon as he stood up to replace the bad wheel with the new one, Zhuang offered to help him, but the craftsman moved him aside:

'Leave it alone! I know my job, you don't.'

He adjusted the wheel, quickly and all by himself.

'How old are you?' Zhuang asked.

'At least seventy.'

'You couldn't find anyone to replace you? It's high time you rested . . .'

'No one, no.'

'You don't have a son?'

'I do, several even.'

'Couldn't you teach them to turn wheels?'

'How? With words? Words can't replace hands. All that's just chatter.'

'What if you showed them?'

'They can't feel the wood. And to work well with wood, you got to have a feel for it.'

'Your knowledge will disappear with you.'

'Like all knowledge.'

The wheelwright eyed his work with a certain pride and turned to Zhuang, holding his gaze:

'Hey, you think you can learn everything in the books of the ancients, right?'

'Yes, you're right, I read our country's sages and thinkers . . .'

'They still exist?'

'They're dead.'

'You walk in their footsteps but they are erased. The dead don't have anything to teach us. What was worthwhile at the time I was born isn't worth a mound of beans today.'

Zhuang meditated on the old wheelwright's lesson. He concurred that words could put us to sleep and spare us from understanding; they freeze a moment and cannot restore the slow movement of things. Birds warble, but what are they saying? Does an eagle speak like a sparrow? Perhaps birdsongs are reduced to the essential, they express fear or love, or warning: watch out, I spotted a hunter in ambush, pointing his crossbow at our clouds, or I saw seeds, or a fire. Do we say anything else? Often, we speak to make noise and exist through this noise. Many events are not translatable into words. The past conditions us, the old wheelwright explained. What if the ancient sages were just dreadful babblers? We are a jumble of acquired experiences and archaic impulses, and words always obey rigid conventions that remove us from a reality in permanent mutation. What I'm speaking about in conventional terms is already no longer the same. It's better to show than tell, since the world is a mess.

Around this time, Master Houei often came up to visit Zhuang. You could see him from far off, on his horse under the yellow parasol and the valet hovering over. Each played his instrument, then drank wine from the calabash and conversed in the silence of the evening, when the peasant women were plucking plants for dye. Both condemned the doctrinal quarrels Zhuang had witnessed for a long time in Linzi, without understanding a thing. Those venerable men who argued away as if in a babble contest were shrinking, reduced to the level of their speeches. They were addicted. And could only fathom things their way and claim to distinguish truth from all that was false in this ever-changing reality. Now, Zhuang understood that nothing was true and nothing was false. Words were like folding screens; one simply had to find the right way of *doing*.

'You're really lucky not to live in the city any more,' Master Houei said. 'In Mong, there is now an inn where important rhetoricians congregate and juggle with words. Honestly! They shine for an audience of boobies.'

'What do they say?'

'They don't say anything. They talk just to talk, revel in their words, vocalize, dive into the fog. They provoke and annoy but they're admired because they have an answer for everything, they know where the winds come from, why the sky doesn't fall . . .'

'Silly idiots!' Zhuang sneered, pouring a big gulp of wine down his gullet.

'They're showmen. They pronounce definitive phrases—"the sky is as low as the earth", "a white dog is black" or "eggs have feathers" . . .'

Confucius wanted words to have precise meanings, acceptable in any kingdom, but one sophist had sown discord more than the others by claiming in his demonstration that a white horse was not a horse, or a pious son was not a son. In weaving his paradoxes he skilfully played with language because there are no articles in Chinese, and one cannot confuse an object with its qualities. The thinkers in all of China who rejected the regimented words of Confucius were singing his paradoxes.

'Ultimately, they're only games,' Master Houei surmised. 'When I crossed the Wei border to come to Song, there was no use asserting my horse wasn't a horse, the Customs agent didn't want to hear about it. He looked at me as if I were crazy and I was made to pay the tariff on horses . . .'

After the music session, at sunset, as they talked about the superiority of sounds owing to their universal character, Master Houei narrated the story of the monkey farm.

Once upon a time there was a trainer who paraded a troupe of chimpanzees in red costumes and hats around marketplaces. They playacted famous farces on their trestle boards, like *The Mill* or *Three Battles*, to the laughter and applause of the delighted small crowds. With their antics, those apes resembled humans, and the trainer raked in plenty of coins at the end of each show. And then came wars and incursions by bandits who plundered the crops and burned down villages; money became scarce. The trainer banded his troupe at the farmyard where they lived, and told them:

'Ah, my good friends, I am obliged to impose some restrictions. From now on, your meals will consist of three chestnuts in the morning and four in the evening . . .'

'Ooh-ooh-ooh!' screeched the apes, baring their teeth.

'Silence! I heard you and I'm going to do my best to keep you happy. To allay your protest, you will have four chestnuts in the morning and three in the evening.'

'Yes! Bravo!' said the apes, dancing with joy.

In both cases, the chimps were rationed at seven chestnuts a day. What was the reason for the jubilation? Master Houei retired, leaving Zhuang with his head full of conflicting questions. There were several ways to interpret the chimps' turnaround, Zhuang said to himself. Either the apes are fools, or unable to count, or that the chestnuts in the mornings are more gratifying before a day's work, or they simulate a sense of satisfaction to be left in peace, perhaps they want to pay homage to the verbal prowess of their trainer who knew how to get his way with them, or fool them. For this was how, through the modulation of words and a resolute tone of voice, tyrants lulled and deluded their people.

Number Six was returning with a bag of crabs when he spotted Zhuang from afar, motionless before a mulberry tree of the forest. He walked up to him and touched his shoulder casually:

'What are you doing, Mister Supervisor, looking at this mulberry tree like that?'

'I'm trying to forget its name. As long as I know its name, I can't see it.'

Baffled, the child creased his brow. Zhuang's words were disconcerting to him.

CHAPTER THIRTEEN

Morning Cloud

Zhuang led a meditative, pastoral life until he turned thirty. Then everything turned upside down. For a long time, Baron Qiu-Chu had been provoking the silent anger of the lords of Song, who blamed him for selling the country to the King of Qi. Rebellion was in the air. The baron knew it and took elaborate precautions. Wild animals would alert him in his antechamber if an intruder came prowling at night. And when he hosted a gala banquet for his vassals in the province to convince them of the efficacy of his management, he had them searched at the entrance and they were made to leave their weapons with the palace guards. Duke Cheng, the angriest one, was seated next to the baron. As soon as the fish were served, he plunged his hand into the belly of his own fish, pulled a dagger out of it and planted it in the baron's heart. He died with his cheek in the sauce and his eyes, blank. Following the established practice of palace coups, Cheng ascended to the throne quite smoothly, and everyone at the court was pleased since most of the dignitaries retained their attributions. They examined together the best way of loosening the grip Qi had on the country and regaining real autonomy without offending their protector, King Min.

While Chou continued to enjoy his position and his fortune, the threat of approaching old age worried him. He summoned his elder son. Zhuang could not refuse him. So one morning, without the slightest feeling of nostalgia, he entered the great house where he'd lived as a child. Clothed as he was in a wildcat-skin cloak, with his bonnet pulled low on his face, he looked so out of place that despite his name the doormen took him for a peddler and were reluctant to let him in. The family residence had been repainted, embellished and enlarged. Reclining on a mat, his father was waiting for him at the end of a hall with marble columns and red-and-gold ceiling. With a skinny hand full of brown spots, he was stroking his beard as thin and translucent as the slaver of a salangane swallow. Two young women were fanning him. In one corner, seers and apothecaries were preparing herbal potions and fumigants, drowning the room in smoke as dense as autumn fog in the hills. Zhuang sat on the floor and was forced to inhale the fumes which made him cough. In a drawling voice, the patriarch said:

'I'm getting old . . .'

'Like all that surrounds us, Father.'

'This house got younger, not I.'

'Objects can be fixed up better than men, that's why they survive us.'

'Zhuang, by force of circumstance you have become my elder son. I am rich and you are poor.'

'Poor? Not at all! I live in the hills and I am at peace there.'

'You lack ambition . . .'

'I certainly hope so!'

'You pig-headed boy! I have plans for you.'

'I fear them, Father.'

'You are thirty years old, and you must marry to respect our traditions.'

'Now, now! You have three other sons from your new wives.'

'They're too young to inherit from our ancestors. And then, you need an official wife.'

'Father, I know people look down on unmarried men, and one who spurns courtesans is called a lunatic, but I live in perfect harmony with Xing and Ching, the girls you offered me years ago to keep me company on a trip.'

'That does not fit your rank any more.'

'What rank?'

'Get married to please your ancestors, give them a son who will continue the family line.'

'What for?' thought Zhuang. He had abandoned all beliefs and no longer understood the benefits of rites. Of what use were those ancestors who swung on their tablets at the first breeze? A means of prolonging oneself—a puerile way of feeling immortal. Zhuang fell silent and listened to his father.

'You know Yee Chen,' he said as if he were changing the subject.

'No, Father.'

'That's not surprising, you barely know what's happening in the palace any more.'

'There are a thousand more exciting lives in the forest.'

'You young fool! Yee Chen has a solid fortune.'

'Whom did he steal it from?'

'From no one, you insolent idiot! He earned every shilling of it in the salt industry and the cattle business. He does whatever he wants in the palace and besides, he built a mansion for himself next to Duke Cheng's.'

'I imagine he's surrounded by flatterers.'

'He can't stand them—in fact, he scorns them.'

'Well, he's right to beware.'

'I spoke to him about you,' Chou went on.

'Because I'm not a courtier?'

'Exactly! That's what he appreciates.'

'Why do you want me to go to his palace for?'

'To marry his daughter.'

'What?'

'Stop posturing! You can't spend the rest of your life supervising lacquers!'

'That knowledge is just as noble as any other.'

'Think of the alliance of our two families . . .'

'Are you sure this young woman isn't a fox who wants to bewitch me?'

'Now you believe in legends—all of a sudden?'

'What's her name?'

'Chao Yun—Morning Cloud. She's fifteen.'

She looked like the white jade figurine of the Goddess of Mercy he had admired in one of the palace temples. Slender, delicate and fragile, she kept her eyes lowered in her oval face, even when she burst out laughing with her sisters or serving women and her cheeks flushed. Chao Yun was timeless. Zhuang imagined she had always existed, like Heaven and Earth. When she finally consented to raise her eyes to him, he noticed her gentle, far-off gaze; he could sense her vulnerability and that touched him. 'I'll protect you from snakes,' he vowed to her.

Zhuang accepted this marriage, but under conditions: the usual go-between could perform his duty and carry deerskins to his future father-in-law, Yee Chen, and lay out pieces of silk as was customary, but he intended to escape the ceremonial of the court nobility, so restricting. He did, however, offer a goose to his father-in-law to seal their alliance and agreed to let his fiancée bring along two of her serving-women, who would become the second and the third wife as soon as the wedding was solemnized. Everything was set on the day of the wedding planned by the seers and protocol specialists. At the end of the ceremony, he led Chao Yun, veiled in red silk, to the bridal chamber in his father's house. To respect a foolish tradition, friends and family members escorted them to their bed, throwing dried fruit in front of them to ward off evil spirits; they teased the bride, making dirty wisecracks about her budding forms, her waist, her curved legs or her bottom. 'Hey Zhuang! You'll break this little girl into pieces!', 'She's skinny as a marsh mosquito!', 'Your beauty's cross-eyed, can't you see?' Women smeared make-up on her cheeks with a cloth. Even Zhuang, ordinarily so calm, lost his temper and finally drove them away: 'Out! Out! You bunch of barbarians!' When they were finally alone, he held Chao Yun's face in his hands, and said: 'It's over. Those jackals won't bother you any more with their dirty talk!' Chao Yun's eyes were misty. Zhuang took off his tunic: it was much too fine for him, and he felt uncomfortable in it.

A week later, Zhuang went to visit his father-in-law, who offered to share his meal. They both put their hands into the dishes. With his mouth full, Yee Chen pointed at his son-in-law with the bone of the yellow chicken he had been nibbling at:

'I intend to place you at Duke Cheng's side.'

'Me?'

'You'll be one of his counsellors. Of course, you won't necessarily be listened to. He does whatever he pleases.'

'In short, I'll be a figurehead, like a banana tree in his garden . . .'

'Cheng needs my money and I need to know what he intends to do with it.'

'You had me walk down from my hills to turn me into a spy?'

'Today, Zhuang, despite Confucius and his flow of fancy words, old people are respected less than they used to be. You'll be my eyes and ears.'

'In the palace? In a world of artifice, jealousy and malicious gossip? Thanks a lot! What advice should I give, tell me. Sincerity is painful to hear, and I know about all the sages who were punished. One of them was roasted, another had his heart ripped out and still another was chopped to bits and ended up in brine! Others were drawn and quartered, dismembered, or at best, died in prison, or became beggars, or were called mad.'

'Oh!'

Yee Chen looked more closely at his bowl of chick broth and, with two fingers, took a long black hair out of it.

'Summon the first cook! I want him punished for his negligence! I want him dismissed!'

'He is not responsible for this mistake, Noble Yee Chen.'

'How's that, Zhuang?'

'Your first cook has every interest in being blameless. If I were you, I would accuse the second cook instead—he's trying to discredit his colleague to take his place.'

'Ha! ha! You have a logical mind, my boy. Be just as logical when you serve the duke and you will serve me at the same time.'

The duke received Zhuang at the Hall of Jade. He immediately sent away the courtiers and seers swarming around him, persistently bowing and scraping to please him. Alone in private with his likely counsellor, he tried to put him at ease:

'My rich friend, Yee Chen, praised your acumen to the skies. My music master, Houei, told me of the clarity of your views and how disinterested you are. The Supreme Director of Lacquers mentioned how articulate you were. . .'

'I find them quite excessive, Mighty Lord.'

'I don't think so. They also know you are defiant and sometimes quick-tempered. Will you always tell me the truth?'

'I will always speak my truth, since I have no interest in pleasing or displeasing.'

'Excellent!'

They walked up to the terrace. The duke put his hands flat on the parapet and glanced at the other terraces below, into the inner courtyards and the open windows.

'You see that girl in front of the door who's arranging flowers?'

'Of course.'

'You see her long, shining black hair, down to her hips? I'd like to ask my guards to shave her head. Her hair would make a magnificent wig for the duchess.'

'You are distrustful of those near you, Noble Lord, but not enough of yourself.'

'How's that?'

'You want to steal the hair of a pretty neighbour without asking her opinion, nor that of her husband.'

'Hair grows back.'

'Not reputation.'

'Tell me . . .'

'If you give that order, the rumour of your presumptuousness will spread through the palace. Even those you control through your largesse will take advantage of it to do you harm.'

'You don't think they're sincere?'

'Never.'

'But I need to find one who's reliable, someone I can trust completely . . .'

The duke lowered his voice and explained to Zhuang:

'I intend to free myself from King Min's protectorate and I see the only way to do it is finding an ally stronger than he is. I thought of our old friendship with King Hiao and I want to rekindle it. He has an army that has never been vanquished.'

'Would he benefit from an alliance with Song? What do you want to offer him in exchange?'

'A safe passage through our land to go around the kingdom of Qi or at least isolate it. In short, reinforce his domination over the region. Besides, Song is rich. How can I find someone prominent and sincere in my entourage of valets? Someone who will not betray me when he's on a secret mission to Hiao?'

'Listen, My Lord, there may be a simple stratagem that will enable you to identify that rare bird . . .'

Zhuang shared his idea with the duke, who burst out laughing:

'I like your ruse! Tomorrow, we'll put it to work.'

The next morning, like every morning, the court awaited the arrival of Duke Cheng in the throne room, chattering in a low voice. When the chamberlain announced the sovereign, there was instantaneous silence, backs bowed, noses dived towards the floor. Zhuang was present; he could sense the mischievousness under the apparent gravity of the duke. Each minister made his usual report. The minister of Public Granaries and Abundance complained that the taxes on grain weren't coming in as they should; his speech was dragging on when all of a sudden the duke, holding his left wrist with his right hand, gave a cry that froze the assembly:

'My fingernail! I lost a nail!'

'Let's look for it!' said the chamberlain, in a panic.

The venerable ministers in ceremonial costumes, brilliant tunics embroidered in gold thread, found themselves on all fours looking for a transparent fingernail. They were shoving, elbowing and kneeing each other discreetly to be the first when Baron Su stood up, sweating but radiant:

'I found it, Mighty Lord!'

He displayed the nail, waving it about at arm's length. The others got up with a nasty look directed at Baron Su, who was congratulated by the duke. Then the daily ceremony resumed its tedious course for two long hours. Later, once the dignitaries had retired, the duke led Zhuang out on the terrace as the day before.

'Do you think Baron Su is the most devoted to me?' he asked him.

'I see things as they are. That man found a nail you never lost.'

'Well, he ripped out one of his fingernails, which proves he's ready to do a lot to please me.'

'Or rather to triumph over his associates.'

'Doesn't that show a certain courage?'

'No, My Lord, rather a certain spinelessness, with the heart of a tiger.'

'So I cannot send him on an embassy to King Hiao?'

'He would be capable of turning against you if you're not there.'

'What about the others?'

'They crawled to show their good will, they genuinely looked for a fingernail that did not exist. They were simply less clever than Baron Su . . .'

'So there's no one I can trust?'

'No one among your courtiers deserves an embassy as delicate as this one.'

'Yes, there is someone,' Duke Cheng said. 'There is one.'

'Who?'

'You.'

CHAPTER FOURTEEN

The Abominable Shang Yang

Surrounded by archers on horseback as skilful as the Mongols they imitated, Zhuang reached the Qin border in a horse-drawn palanquin. He had travelled for a long time, far too long, with a swan in a gilded cage, a haughty animal he found rather pretentious and to which he had nothing to say. Duke Cheng thought King Hiao would be delighted with such a distinguished present, a swan that had been swimming in a sacred lake until now. This whole mission was far removed from Zuang's tastes and intuitions. Disguised as an ambassador, he felt grotesque, but what else could he do? He had arrived in the state of Qin, located between the Yellow River and the mountains, in the high valley of the Wei River. All of a sudden, his convoy stopped. Zhuang lifted the curtain of his carriage. He saw soldiers of an unknown breed, with long armour in iron plates which made them look like centipedes. These monsters wore epaulettes reinforced by aggressive spikes; they reminded him of the forest apes that bristle up the hair on their huge shoulders to appear terrifying. Because of their accent, Zhuang couldn't understand what they were yapping about but he got down from his palanquin. The archers in his escort had grouped together: they would not intervene to protect him.

'We've been expecting you, Ambassador,' said a little man with a high-pitched voice in a black robe and a hat bordered with fur.

'How did you know I would arrive today?'

'In Qin, we know everything.'

'Who are you?'

'I am Eunuch Zhou.'

'King Hiao is the one who sent you?'

'As your guide, Ambassador. May I climb into your palanquin?'

The question had the tone of an order. Without waiting for an answer, he settled inside, adjusting the cushions; Zhuang followed him. Before he closed the curtains, he noticed his archers' horses were confiscated, and expressed his surprise.

'No worries, Ambassador,' Eunuch Zhou said, sprawled out on the cushions. 'Your men will remain at the border.'

He pointed to a group of shacks at the foot of the rocks, explaining:

'They'll find what they need to eat and drink, and mats to rest on. Armed foreigners are forbidden to enter our territory and anyone who wants to settle in Qin or even pass through, must be inscribed in our register. Your name is already there, Ambassador.'

'Many people come to Qin?'

'No one. They know how harsh we are, no one wants to immigrate here. Our laws are too severe.'

He let out a shrill laugh that stopped abruptly when he shouted an order through the closed curtain:

'Let's go!'

Zhuang took advantage of the ride to the capital to learn about the country. Eunuch Zhou was garrulous:

'Our country has improved over the last ten years. The bandits have disappeared. Disagreements are no longer settled by violence. Weights and measures have been standardized. Arable plots of land now have boundaries. Each province is required to feed fifty thousand inhabitants. Besides that, the peasants supply the army with grain and fodder.'

'Your vision is idyllic, it reminds me of Confucius. He achieved similar results by setting the example of his perfect honesty. When he was Minister of Crime under Duke Ting, crimes and debauchery had come to an end.'

'The bandits had not disappeared,' Zhou went on, 'They were plotting. The neighbouring states of Lu, where he was trying out his policy of goodness, succeeded in bribing Duke Ting by sending him young girls and superb horses to lure him away from Confucius who execrated this kind of corruption. Confucius resigned. It is not enough to set an example, my friend.'

Eunuch Zhou detailed the measures that had made Qin's fortune. The people were divided into groups of villages whose inhabitants had to be responsible for each other, as much in their work as in their abjection. Everyone was to warn the local authorities of an offense committed by a neighbour or a brother, or else he was beheaded. Turning in a relative received the same honours as those given to a soldier for his valiance. The army was also divided into brigades of five men—if one deserted, the other four were executed. 'That's why we have very few deserters.'

'I see,' Zhuang said. 'In your country, fear reigns better than elsewhere.'

'With many advantages. A civil servant who denounces his superior replaces him.'

'I know the drill,' Zhuang sighed.

'That drill is effective. A peasant who produces more than the required quota is exempted from corvées.'

'How about the one who produces less?'

'He's made a slave,' Zhuang answered, laughing.

'So denunciation is the norm . . .'

'Yes, and children are valuable to us for this type of job. They never hesitate to tell us their parents' turpitudes.'

Zhuang remained immersed in his thoughts. At nightfall, the soldiers were lighting torches that made their metallic armour gleam with a flickering orange glint. Zhuang peeked outside his carriage. They had arrived at the Hulao Pass, the spot from where Confucius' contemporary Lao-Tzu had disappeared for ever, astride a blue water-buffalo. Old Lao, they say, had been a curator at the Royal Library of Chu; revolted by the stupidity of men, he had decided to abandon his position and escape. A guard at the pass recognized Lao and asked him to write a book for him; Lao dictated five thousand words to the guard who transcribed them. Zhuang never had the scrolls of this famous book in his hands, but wandering scholars had recited many of its maxims to him. Zhuang liked the extravagance and strangeness of this Lao-Tzu, with his concision that often verged on obscurity. He recited one of Lao's maxims under his breath.

'The more laws, the more bandits . . .'

'What are you saying?' Zhou asked.

'Nothing, I'm saying nothing, I'm just humming,' Zhuang replied.

In the morning, they arrived before the new walls of Xianyang, the capital of Qin. This city had been built with masonry ramparts, donjons, towers, a monumental portcullis at the great gate decorated with the trophies of war, flags, weapons captured from enemies whose decapitated heads had been buried under the soft earth of the moats. The city was as square as a military camp, deserted, and palaces gave way to barracks but you couldn't tell one from the other, so severe were their facades. Zhuang got off his palanquin after Zhou, who carried the caged swan put to sleep by the swinging of the wheels. Zhuang considered the height of the building:

'Does King Hiao live here?'

'No.'

'Yet I have come to visit him.'

'You will not see him, Ambassador.'

'But I must negotiate for Duke Cheng!'

'No one can see the king.'

'So where are we going?'

'We're going to the Great Creator of Good.'

'That is?'

'Prince Shang Yang, to whom we owe our unyielding fortune, incomparable strength, and above all, our law'

'He replaced King Hiao?'

'The king, may Heaven protect him, expresses himself through the prince's mouth.'

'Is he his son? His heir?'

'He's Shang Yang, to whom we owe . . .'

'I know. What about my swan? What should I do with my swan?'

'I'm keeping it. The Great Creator of Good will feast on a broth made with its filets and its carcass.'

'A sacred swan?'

'Sacred in Song. Here only the law is sacred.'

Eunuch Zhou guided Zhuang through the interior of the immense, empty palace, with its bare walls. No guards anywhere. Zhou was silent, for the slightest whisper would echo through the corridors and nothing was supposed to disturb the perfect silence of the place. Zhuang was following his guide through this maze when a door opened and he saw Shang Yang, standing with his hands on his hips. He was waiting for him in a room furnished with just one lacquered armchair.

The prince was of short stature but muscular as a logger, slightly bowed, with hooked moustaches, a short, tough beard, unusual for a Chinese man, and very black hair, as black as his tunic. There were no colours in Qin: black was further enhanced by contrast with the white of the walls and the metallic grey of the armours. Through the wooden latticed window, the dark-blue sky shed light on an ash-coloured land. Zhuang bowed and the Prince said to him:

'What have you come to ask for, Zhuang Zhou?'

'Great Creator of Good, Song needs your support . . .'

'What is your little kingdom offering me? What strange deal are you proposing?'

'You could have advanced posts in our country, along the border we have in common with Qin . . .'

'So what? Wei does, too. All my armies have to do is flow into the lower plains to devour Wei and follow our policy of eastern expansion, as our late Duke Miu had wished. Wei controls the Yellow River and the mountains of the East. Do I need authorization? But you must be hungry after your trip.'

Shang Yang clapped his hands. A swarm of servants invaded the room, unrolled carpets and mats, set up low tables and dishes made of translucent horn.

'Let's talk,' said the Prince.

He half lay down to taste his bowl. Zhuang imitated him.

'Delicious, His Excellency, truly delicious.'

'It's panther foetus.'

The moment seemed propitious, so Zhuang continued:

'So I won't see King Hiao?'

'What for? You're seeing me. You know, what makes a king is his position, not his qualities. He must remain invisible, preserved from everyone and everything. With no tastes, no intentions, no anger, no ideas. He only exists to personify the law. And what about you, who seem such an unlikely emissary?'

'Oh, me! Let's say I'm a man of letters with no particular function, who is being used.'

'I distrust rhetoricians and those wandering men of letters who acquire offices. We crack down on those parasites whose speeches weaken the nation! Men of letters are incapable of hearing new ideas, they live in the knowledge of their old books, they can only perform menial tasks. Intelligence is evil. I want to rule over an inert people.'

'The good of the State can be an evil for the people, Prince.'

'The people! An educated people is dangerous. One doesn't rule by knowledge but by force. You believe in the Golden Age, eh?'

'When people were content with little? Certainly.'

'Nonsense! Now I look at the world as it is. And it is overpopulated. I must make it toe the line. To help agriculture thrive, we need war. In times of peace, parasites help themselves. Peace means surplus, and surplus attracts sharks!'

'Can one live in a constant state of war?'

'Yes. Warring peoples dominate others. I want to make my people love war, the only way to obtain rewards.'

The servants kept bringing in delicacies. Zhuang filled his belly with a gluttony that expressed itself in little chuckles punctuating Shang Yang's disturbing monologue. He claimed that asking a people to come up with a policy was impossible as they would be too dependent on their impulses and their whims; they could hardly rejoice at the successes of their king. To gather people around him, Shang advocated calling on the basic selfishness of men:

'Only self-interest guides them, Ambassador, not the ravings of your Confucius. The baker doesn't make bread for his own pleasure but to make money—otherwise he'd give it away for free.'

'So the law only serves to hold them together,' Zhuang said with a full mouth.

'The law,' the prince continued, 'must become our second nature. For that it must be simple, clear, and all of a piece. That's why we must promulgate prohibitions and increase the punishment for minor offenses in order to eradicate major ones.'

Zhuang did not answer. He was taking in the prince's words with his cheeks puffed up by a sublime hare compote seasoned with mountain herbs.

'Moral values are artificial,' Prince Shang continued. 'It's better to condition the people's reflexes! Virtue is only a disguise for self-interest! Make humanity more stupid! The people's intelligence is so limited that those who work for its good are rejected. Believe me, those brutes only obey a tamer!'

CHAPTER FIFTEEN

How Zhuang Got Out of a Tight Spot

Zhuang should have gone into hiding or disappear to avoid this futile deputation. With these mad principles of the Prince of Qin, he was running a real risk. In troubled, unstable times, one must retreat into silence, stay put, remain inconspicuous, protect oneself from the powers that be. Utter not a word, not a sound, content oneself with one's garden and the natural music from the cascades. Zhuang did not have the courage to slip away and he cursed himself for it. A remnant of rites and traditions, reverence for the ancients, politeness, all that rubbish had paralysed him. He had let his family direct his life without ever giving his opinion. In fact, he was a victim of circumstances and had no opinion about anything.

He was dreaming distractedly about these things while Eunuch Zhou showed him the installations of Qin, all military, from combat exercises to the siloes being filled by peasants lined up like insects with their backs bent under sacks, or pushing carts ahead of them. They weren't really men any more. And Zhou explained what he had already realized: Shang wanted to unify China by devouring its kingdoms piece by piece; he no longer wished to govern a parcel of territory but a whole empire.

Zhuang pretended to listen to Zhou's lullaby, but he was thinking: 'When you think you've succeeded in achieving some kind of serenity, the social conventions pop up to stop you.' Duke Cheng had lacked sensitivity when he chose him as an ambassador; Zhuang had neither the easy-going directness nor the calculating mind that would enable him to say one thing instead of another, or feign admiration before a madman.

'I'll walk you to your quarters,' Zhou said. 'We'll leave for your border tomorrow at dawn. Get some rest.'

While shutting the massive wooden door of the large, round bedroom where he had taken Zhuang, the eunuch was still smiling as he had all day long. He pushed the latch of the door to lock it like in a prison. The vexed ambassador felt caged. He looked around the room, saw the recesses in the walls masked by curtains, barred windows that gave onto ponds and courtyards. In the middle, a rather rudimentary mat, and on a stand, a bowl overflowing with fruit next to a pitcher, which he sniffed: it was wine. He was about to drink some when, behind him, drawing one of the curtains, a young man in a tunic embroidered with birds, carrying a squirrel on his shoulder held by a little golden chain, told him in a soft but imperious voice:

'Don't drink!'

Zhuang put the pitcher down; the young man walked over, picked it up and poured a puddle of wine onto the floor; then he lifted his squirrel by the skin of its back and held its muzzle down against the puddle. The animal drank.

'Your squirrel seems to like my wine . . .'

'Be patient,' the young man said.

The animal was playing at rolling a fruit over the floor when it stiffened, sat up on its hind legs, turned on itself and collapsed. The young man took Zhuang by the arm:

'Hurry up now!'

He raised the wall hanging through which he had entered; it concealed another door, a smaller one, from which sprang five men in black robes carrying an inert body. They deposited the body on the mat without excessive precautions. On a gesture from the young man, Zhuang was made to take off his ambassadorial clothes and they dressed the corpse in them. He quickly put on a black tunic, typical of Qin. The men staged the scene: one of them emptied the pitcher of wine through the window and put it on its side next to the nightstand; another got rid of the squirrel's corpse and returned the golden chain to the young man. Then all of them disappeared as they had entered, in silence. The young man held Zhuang back behind the curtain, motioning him to remain still and peek through the half-open door. Shortly afterward, soldiers filled the room, leaned over the body, turned it over to be sure it was dead and took it away without locking the door behind them.

'Luckily,' Zhuang said, 'The eunuch wasn't with them. He would have realized immediately the bodies had been switched.'

'Those jobs are not part of his role. What counts is that you're dead.'

'Tell me, you didn't save me for nothing.'

'True. Are you familiar with the *Classic of Poetry*? 'Even rats know how to behave, but there are men who do not. Why are they not soon dead? The man who alienates others will fall.'

Zhuang followed the young man down a steep staircase. He introduced himself as the son of King Hiao. Shang could not get at him without attracting the sovereign's wrath, so he was content to keep him isolated. He had his tutor, Master Jia, convicted of corruption; they tattooed his forehead like a criminal and he was now rotting in jail. His other preceptor had his nose cut off.

'When my father disappears, so will Shang. Let me tell you—no one will protect him because everyone holds a grudge against him.'

'At the moment, I'm the one who had to disappear.'

'He told you too much, and immediately regretted it. That corpse the soldiers picked up—they will decapitate it, put it in your palanquin, and it will join the bodies of your coachman and archers. That crew will be deposited on the other side of our border. The soldiers will pillage and burn a village or two. They'll accuse bandits of the crime and no embassy will ever have taken place.'

'How did Shang Yang rise to the top?'

'Through luck and intrigue, for the man's one sly devil. He's not from here, as you might have realized from his accent. He's from Wei.'

The conversation continued at the palace of the young heir, over a great deal of unpoisoned wine. Zhuang was recovering from his latest adventures by learning about the origin and ascent of Prince Shang Yang, the son of a royal concubine. At twenty, he served the Prime Minister, who had noticed his lively mind and lack of scruples. When the minister fell ill, he confided to Shang:

'I'm too weak for such a heavy task. I would like you to replace me.'

'Did you tell the king?'

'I told him he must either employ Shang or kill him—you must prevent Shang from serving some other king.'

'If the King of Wei doesn't agree when you advise him to employ me, he may listen to you when you ask him to kill me . . .'

Shang Yang changed kingdoms and offered his services to King Hiao of Qin. He charmed the King by cautioning him not to model himself after what was old: 'Some dynasties have died out from not having reformed rites.' He entrusted his kingdom to Shang so the principles of the School of Jurists could be implemented. Shang was cruel, intransigent and authoritarian, but seeing his results, the king trusted him . . .

Later that evening, Zhuang and the heir apparent drank themselves to sleep.

CHAPTER SIXTEEN

The Revenant

King Hiao's son contrived a tiger hunt to help Zhuang return to the border. They had him dressed as a pikeman. He had to wear a heavy helmet that was too big and its visor kept falling on his nose. Under a large cape with a moleskin collar, he wore a coat of mail that went down to his shins. Eunuch Zhou, his guide from the day before, would be unlikely to recognize him. The weather was clear, but dark clouds were piling up in the east. Zhuang went back on the road that had led him to Shang Yang's palace. Standing in the young man's chariot, the ride seemed interminable, but he felt safe amidst a small group of hunters loyal to the crown prince. No one said a word until they reached the border. Zhuang finally recognized the shacks where he'd been forced to leave his archers. The convoy stopped and he got off the chariot with aching muscles. He left his pike in the case of the vehicle, took off his helmet and chainmail but kept the coat.

'I still can't understand why you saved me,' he told the prince. 'Yesterday, you answered evasively by quoting the *Classic of Poetry*...'

'Do not try to understand everything.'

'I'm still curious.'

'Go now! I have to kill a tiger.'

Be they slayers or saviours, the powerful never answer questions, why bother asking them? Zhuang watched the young prince lead his warriors into the depths of the forest that opened beyond a rockslide. He turned around and began walking southeast towards his city of Mong. Stifling his anger, he only let it surge in slight jolts.

Zhuang swore he would never again rub shoulders with men in power, never seek their support or their flattering company, never become their valet or their buffoon. He vowed to never obey again. He was discovering that the government of individuals suppressed individuals by multiplying restrictions. He had listened attentively to what Shang Yang said and he was shaken by it. One could only rule by violence, explicit or tacit, nevertheless palpable, formidable and contemptuous. By extending control into households where sons denounced their fathers. From now on, Zhuang resolved to live apart so as not to be ashamed to live. Shang Yang's words had given him a glimpse of the worst. Would he want a world where leisure was forbidden and forced labour the norm? The desire to do nothing was already called laziness. Laze rhymes with sage—Zhuang hummed to a familiar tune and he rolled in the grass of the meadows bellowing with laughter to celebrate his freedom.

He walked on for three whole months, dawdling, open to chance encounters, never asking his way, certain that he would arrive somewhere. He fed on fruits and roots, except when villagers invited him into their homes—one offered a bag of dried meat, another a gourd of wine in a goatskin. Free of all constraints, Zhuang kept walking. One evening, holding on to sweet-smelling bushes along a steep, perilous path with a torrent down below, he fell upon a small hut made of rushes. He sat inside to catch his breath and thought of spending the night there. He heard the melancholy cry of a wild goose that warned of coming rain. Sheltered by a kind of awning made of lotus leaves, he wrapped himself in his cloak and set his head on a stone.

'You're right to take shelter, stranger, it's going to come down hard tonight.'

Zhuang sat up and saw a gnome walking on his hands and knees, agile as a toad, which he actually resembled: a big mouth, fat cheeks, bulging eyes and a jumping body.

'My name is Yun Chong—In the Midst of Clouds,' the gnome said, 'And I bid you welcome. Yes, I know, a judge had my feet cut off because I was trying to evade taxes, but I got used to it and that doesn't stop me from roaming in the woods, and then, I'm happy living over this torrent. Hey, look down, I built a little dam to stop fish. It's my fish-tank. I draw on it all year long.'

Zhuang remained with the toad-man for a week. At first, they only talked about ways of surviving in the wild—brutal, yes, but less so than the world of humans, for it is less perverted by cunning and manoeuvres; a world guileless, elemental. Animals rarely killed for the taste of blood, except for tigers, whose murderous instinct they evoked; but despite the snakes, the stagnant waters, the brambles and the rugged, dangerous landscapes, nature was generous when you knew how to caress it. The toad-man was agile, even if he couldn't stand on his feet any more, or perhaps more so for that very reason. He taught Zhuang the art of trapping and making a bow out of bamboo to hunt birds. Showed him how to run through the rocks better than an ibex, scale cliffs by pulling yourself up by the arms and sense the coming of a storm by watching ants. He introduced him to medicinal plants, the ones grey monkeys chew to prevent migraines or heal their wounds. The toad-man kept a fire perpetually lit for warmth and for grilling fish. They talked before the rekindled flames at nightfall, resting after their runs through the mountains or the nearby forest. It took a few days before they talked about themselves:

'If I had stayed in the village,' the toad-man said, 'I would have been a beggar. Kids would throw stones at me to poke fun at my painful faces and some would curse me for this mutilation they'd see as the punishment for a crime. My crime? Oh! I had hidden the provisions I refused to give up as taxes. Here, at least, I'm my own master. And you're my first visitor.'

In his turn, Zhuang recounted his misadventures comically, and they joked about them.

'Your princes, like my peasants, live on prejudice.'

'I'm afraid so,' Zhuang said. 'We must unlearn all systems of thought, prejudice, angry moods and comparisons. I have learnt to my cost that rituals divide us and give rise to violence.'

'I, too, know that when justice wants to impose goodness, it gives rise to violence in a similar way.'

'I have learnt,' Zhuang added, 'that misfortune comes from the honours that make us vain, and that fame provokes fear.'

'Ah, yes!' the toad-man continued, 'Most men live in fear out of their need to conform. Conformism! Even Confucius was a conformist. He stopped on the way, never went beyond it.'

'Not so sure,' Zhuang answered, adamantly defending the old master. 'Confucius modified his teaching according to his interlocutors—he held back some and pushed others forward.'

They spent the night holding forth on beliefs, prejudice and conformism. They agreed on the perils of convictions which remove us from reality and, in the end, are merely distractions.

When Zhuang went back down towards the valleys of Song, the fog setting in on the rocky foothills followed his steps, protecting him as if to prevent him from turning back. He then understood the toad-man's nickname, Yun Chong, 'In the Midst of Clouds'. His stay in the hut made of rushes had been beneficial: from now on, he would be able to cope in the wilderness. His feeling of having no convictions had been strengthened. He thought of his new friend whom he would never see again. Yun Chong viewed things with a neutral eye, refrained from reducing them to a discourse; showing them was enough for him. Fortunately, he had nothing to demonstrate. All men seemed superficial in comparison with him and his exemplary life. They drown themselves in work, noise, images and distractions. Solitude terrifies them; they need excess because they fear emptiness: they have no idea of its appeasing properties. As he walked, Zhuang made a resolution: 'I want to look at the world without preconceived notions, as if it were always new, yet to be discovered, and ceaselessly surprising. I want to let myself be astonished and banish my memory. I want to be empty.'

As he walked lightly over the hills, he could see, down in the plain, cultivated squares of farmland that had destroyed nature, encroaching upon the vast primeval forests that had to be cleared by fire so that more and more inhabitants could feed themselves. Men had been domesticated at the same time as nature. Zhuang knew farmers were subjected to taxes and forced labour and sometimes sent off to war; they didn't have the freedom of the hunter in the mountains who was familiar with plants and asparagus roots. 'Heaven decrees no law,' Zhuang thought, 'and yet one season follows another.'

It was autumn. The wind rose; it would blow for weeks. Zhuang took advantage of a yellow sandstorm to join a caravan of merchants on their way to Mong. All of them were powdered with sand and protected their faces, especially their eyes, under cloths,. They resembled each other like a procession of yellow-dyed statues. They could hardly identify each other as they walked along, sheltered by their squeaking carts, subjected to the assaults of the wind. Zhuang held firmly on to the sides of a tarpaulin clacking in the wind and almost flying off at each gust. They advanced blindly. After some trying hours, the caravan reached the gates of the city where they could better shelter themselves. The ramparts stopped the gusts of wind but the warm, stinging sand was whirling in the narrow streets. Many of them took a rest, squatting along the walls; they brushed away the sand from their clothing and hair with their hands. His coat floating around him like a sail, Zhuang walked towards the palace of his fabulously rich father-in-law.

The huge building was abandoned to an untidy army of workers. In the whirlwinds of sand entering the city, masked carpenters were playing acrobats, hanging onto the facade to patch up the openings. Zhuang took advantage of the construction site to slip inside, pretending to help carry boards. In the inner courtyard, a foreman armed with a whip was shouting himself hoarse to his teams of workers:

'You men there, with your boards, quick! Go upstairs!'

Zhuang went with the flow and while his chance companions were lugging their loads to the windows that weren't boarded up yet while others were tying up the wooden slats tightly. He wandered through the gallery that led to the former quarters of Chao Yun. Zhuang had returned because of her, because he had promised to protect her and refused to go back on his word. Often in his dreams, he imagined her next to him in the country. As ill-luck would have it, he passed by one of the butlers he knew, who insulted him, at first:

'Go back with the others, you bum!'

'No,' Zhuang said.

'What? What? You got no business here in this part of the palace of the Honourable Yee Chen!'

'Oh yes I do . . .'

'A thief? Get out of here, or I'll yell!'

The butler raised his eyes to Zhuang, who was shaking the sand off his hair. He opened his eyes wide and stood there gaping. When his fright grew stronger than the paralysis caused by stupor, he ran out, bellowing:

'A ghost! A ghost!'

Zhuang followed him, but he was in no hurry. At the end of the gallery, a group of men emerged suddenly from a salon, led by the master of the palace, Yee Chen, who believed in his gold more than in revenants.

'Zhuang!' he said. 'You're not dead?'

'As you can see. My head's on my shoulders, I can move my arms and legs. And I'm hungry and thirsty.'

Yee Chen sent away the men accompanying him, and pushed Zhuang into an empty room. There, he explained the whole story to him. They had found his body not far from the Qin border, nailed to the wood of his palanquin by a lance. His archers had been killed, his coachman, too. They had all been decapitated by a horde of the brigands who were burning villages and devastating the north of Song.

'They recognized me without my head?' Zhuang joked?

'Your clothing had the ambassadorial coat of arms emblazoned on it. Duke Cheng gave the order to bury you in the cemetery of the North, but on the sly, since your mission was to remain secret. That was over three months ago . . .

Zhuang narrated to him all that had happened in the country of Shang Yang, and how the crown prince of Qin had saved him. He then told him of his wanderings. He said he had been extremely reluctant to return, but he had to because of Chao Yun.

'She's in mourning for you,' Yee Chen said.

'Seeing me again should make her happy.'

'Or frighten her!'

'No, I've come to take her with me, Noble Yee Chen.'

'To take her where? In the woods? My daughter's not a savage!'

'She's my wife.'

'The wife of a dead man! Even your family can do nothing for her. Your father died, too, when he learnt that bandits had murdered you. He turned red and collapsed.'

'He was old. Even trees die when their time comes.'

'You and your father are both in your family altar.'

'I am delighted to know that.'

'You can't stay here, Zhuang, you can't show yourself to the duke as a revenant. I'll get you out of Mong and send you to one of my distant villas. Here, we must forget you.'

'So be it, but first . . .'

'You'll take your wife and her servants. Her absence will seem normal, after her sorrow.'

'Yes, but first I wouldn't mind having something to eat.'

'You have a good appetite for a dead man.'

'I quite like the position of dead man. No need to be accountable for anything, no more bowing to anybody, no more rites to observe. All that was insignificant. Up until now, my life was based on things of no importance.'

'What is important, Zhuang?'

'Heaven.'

CHAPTER SEVENTEEN

Beneficial Drunkenness

As they went through the fence of plum trees and climbing plants of
the Pavilion of the Green Torrent, Chao Yun and Zhuang had no idea
they would have to spend several years there. The name of the local-
ity was inaccurate. The torrent had been tamed by a series of small
cascades, and Lord Yee Chen had added several long buildings with
visible frameworks to the original pavilion; beams, joists, pillars and
exposed frames were painted, oval doors and round windows opened
the walls under curved roofs with turned-up angles in golden-yellow
or dark-purple polished tiles. Two friendly bearded dragons, their
claws planted in the earth, kept watch over the main entrance. The
buildings melded into the garden where you could sense an extreme
aversion for straight lines, too. Here, duckweed put a white touch on
the ditches, there, red wisteria hung from rocks cut out of the mountain. The famous pavilion now stood proudly in the middle of an artificial lake, accessible only by boat. The chrysanthemums were in full
autumnal bloom, and an inseparable couple of mandarin ducks
swam negligently about. Chao Yun found them endearing. At the

Pavilion, Zhuang immediately rediscovered his taste for idleness. The harmony of this disorderly decor contributed to his inclination and, little by little, with light touches, he began to organize his feelings.

Together, they settled in.

They had to move the contents of the wagons they had brought along into the Pavilion of the Green Torrent: tunics, furniture with mother-of-pearl inlay, makeup, perfumes, gilt-wood statuettes. Zhuang disapproved of these unnecessary luxuries, but he let Chao Yun do as she wished, for she needed to be surrounded by familiar objects. Zhuang liked the peace of this secluded spot, even though the low bows of the numerous staff bothered him right away. Gardeners, cooks, handmaids—he wanted to raise them to his level but they refused, jealously guarding their functions, happy to work for such a rich entrepreneur as Yee Chen. Zhuang realized that he came very rarely and the servants had all the time to organize themselves, or more precisely, to loaf around all year long and take advantage of their good fortune. In short, they were the real masters. With the gardeners, Zhuang talked harmony. He asked them to fill out a bush of bamboos or trim the willow tree so he could savour the full moon from his round window. With the cooks, he spoke like an expert. While he could easily make do with herbs and roots from the forest, he did not spurn the soft-shelled clams dug up in the fogs of the Yellow River, nor the fried bee chrysalides; he relished the fresh bamboo shoots that felt firm under your teeth and the crunchy duck gizzards, and he had these delicacies in mind when he visited the farmyard. He simply wanted his staff to feast as well as he did, for power in all its forms was odious to him.

Nonetheless, he adapted to the circumstances. In the morning, wrapped up with Chao Yun in a tapir fur, he accepted fried rice with ginger in a bowl of boiling water and then, reinvigorated by this tonic brew, he sometimes walked to the nearby village of Tong-Ha, little houses aligned along the southern banks of the Yellow River. The fishermen were mending their nets and Zhuang had many conversations with them. He enjoyed their terse, concrete way of speaking and soaked it up. While he called them his friends, once he turned his back, they called him the Lord of the Pavilion. They made fun of him, but indulgently, for they didn't quite understand his strange ideas. One day, seeing fish swim in a large bucket before they were sold, Zhuang exclaimed:

'That's the pleasure of fish!'

'You ain't no fish,' an old toothless fisherman replied, smiling.

'You're not me.'

'That's true, all right.'

'So how do you know I don't know what the pleasure of fish is?'

'I'm not you, but you're not a fish. Fish don't wear tunics.'

'Prejudice!'

Zhuang sent some of his servants out to buy all the fish that had just come out of the Yellow River and had them thrown into his lake where he watched them swim. He envied their nonchalance.

When spring returned, Zhuang was awakened at dawn by a blackbird that interpreted a different score every time. Crickets repopulated the weeping willow. He often took Chao Yun to the lake and the dew would wet her black tunic; he had persuaded her that dark cloth accentuated her light skin. They would go to the rowboats and while she relaxed at the prow in the early sunlight, Zhuang took the oars. An empty boat, possibly released from its anchor by a gust of wind, knocked against theirs and he pushed it away with his hand.

'If a boat with people on board had hit us,' she said, 'You would have insulted the rower!'

'You are right, because he would either be an egoist who doesn't care about others, or an incompetent who doesn't know how to row. I can't accuse a gust of wind.'

'But the careless rower wouldn't necessarily wish to harm.'

'All I ask of him is to be good at what he does.'

At that time, they made themselves a kind of nest on the covered terrace of the Pavilion, sheltered from the sun that rose to heat the earth. There, in a completely relaxed atmosphere, they practiced the art of caresses. Detached from the negative desires brought out by conflicts, Chao Yun and Zhuang lived in a healthy, joyful surge of communion with nature. She would turn pink, with her eyes closed, her ears burning and her nostrils flaring. They paused, and then resumed their tender movements. Their embrace was the marriage of fire and water, speed and slowness, earth and sky. Fulfilled and exhilarated, they would return to the Pavilion.

At other times, Zhuang took refuge on the top of a tower from where he could see the countryside all the way to the southern bed of the Yellow River. He replayed in his mind the situations that had led him to the Pavilion of the Green Torrent. And was amused by the idea that his father's second family were sacrificing suckling pigs for him while his ghost was in such wonderful health. Then he'd wonder again why Shang Yang hadn't simply cut his throat—why the complicated staging? Perhaps to signal that in Qin, brigands didn't dare burn down a single cottage and that, in comparison, Song was quite weak. Here, at least, the wine wasn't poisoned, and Zhuang drank large glassfuls of it every day, until he got into a foggy trance. In that state, he could focus on minute details, without a single thought in his head. Thanks to his drunkenness, he could forget the walls of the tower, forget the landscape, forget himself even as he fell back onto the cushions and began to snore blissfully.

One evening, as he was far into his drunken state, Chao Yun's voice shook him out of his torpor. He got up on shaky legs, holding on to a beam, and shouted he was coming. What did she want to tell or show him? He had no idea. It was enough to hear the sound of her voice and he didn't want to make her wait. He ventured down the narrow wooden stairs, unsteady on his feet, hesitating over every step, his head spinning. Never mind . . . He concentrated on his legs, held on to the bumps on the wall, went down one floor, staggered, held back, began the descent to the first floor, and there—was it because of a brief dizzy spell—he missed a step, his foot skidded and he tumbled downstairs, bumping elbows and knees on the staircase, sliding every which way over the floor. Chao Yun panicked and called for help. Her handmaids rushed over to Zhuang's prostrate body and turned him over. He was laughing heartily. With his hands flat on the floor and his arms outstretched, he sat up. Chao Yun squatted next to him:

'You're not hurt, are you? Nothing broken?'

'Broken? No, no. The wine helped. Had I been sober and missed a step I'd have tried to hold myself back. I would have resisted the fall, tumbled the wrong way, banged against the edge of a step and I might have broken my neck. But see, the wine made me pliant. Instead of resisting, I went with the fall and I didn't hurt myself in the slightest.'

CHAPTER EIGHTEEN

The Valley of the Four Winds

Over the years Zhuang had given up flutes and citharas because their predictable music no longer pleased him. Chao Yun was baffled by this: he used to play the traditional melodies so delicately. As she expressed her surprise, he explained that he had heard the music of the earth, so much more powerful than music humans could produce. She still didn't understand, so he decided to take her above the Valley of the Four Winds, where he retreated more and more often. Very early in the morning, he had a quadriga made ready and wanted to drive it himself. The excursion began with a bumpy ride over the meadows. They stopped at a peasant village, a cluster of dried mud huts with holes made by shrews and palm leaves for roofs. Zhuang took his walking stick and ordered the peasants who came to him to help carry Chao Yun up to the higher hills. A tall farmer with a fixed, silly smile wrapped the young woman in a piece of cloth and hoisted her up on his back like a bundle. Then they climbed up the difficult, steep path that led to the summit. When they reached a platform that looked out over the valley, they sat there and contemplated the thousand nuances of the landscape, from a luminous green like parrot feathers to the deep green of the junipers bearing dark-blue fruit. The porter lay down for a nap with his bamboo hat over his nose, while Zhuang asked his companion:

'What do you see in this valley?'

'A forest . . .'

'No. It's an orchestra. When the earth breathes, it plays a symphony. You have to wait for the wind to rise, and here it rises every evening. Then it speaks, it whispers, it shouts, it modulates its voice as it slips into the foliage, it crashes against the tree-trunks and sets off again to growl at the foot of the hills, it whistles, it bellows . . .'

To enjoy the unexpected sounds of this orchestra more fully, Zhuang showed Chao Yun how to create a void inside oneself. You had to rid your mind of your intentions, interrupt your movements, and then listen to yourself breathing, listen to your breath becoming calm, slowing down and becoming imperceptible. When the outside world faded out, calm started to fill them. They were free of care, vacant, open to anything, and more receptive.

The wind rose at twilight.

First, a swell bent the tall grass before slipping to the foot of the hills. The breeze caressed the cliffs facing them and sounded like flutes; the wind was now shivering over the lotus leaves, playing between the needles of the pine trees, tousling the willows like the hair of mad dancing girls. An ample sound from far away was becoming distinct. Where the forest grew scarce, the dull notes of the wind were beating the wide leaves and making the smallest ones tinkle like little bells at the bottom of the tree trunks. On the leaves already dry, the sound turned into a wail, and when it licked the caves open like mouths on the face of the cliffs, out came a rumbling of drums. Zhuang sighed:

'Ah, celestial music is something else altogether, but should we seek to know what is beyond our knowledge?'

CHAPTER NINETEEN

Illumination

Zhuang had lost the notion of time. His existence was sewed together by little, unimportant things that fulfilled him. He'd had the leisure to teach Chao Yun the exquisite pleasures of writing in Chinese script, which she had now mastered. Contrary to the times, which demanded that she be a weaver or mistress of culinary ceremonies, she helped him in his intensive studies of the life of animals and plants, thus extending the initiatory lessons of Yun Chong, the toad-man. Together, by the trembling candle of a Chinese lantern, they recorded their observations on scrolls piled up in racks that ran along all the free walls of the tower. They rarely heard from the outside world but it didn't bother them, except when Yee Chen came to visit at the end of spring. There would be a great commotion at the Pavilion of the Green Torrent at these times. The staff was forced to bustle about and busy themselves with a hundred tasks to show the master how useful they were. Zhuang was not fond of these visits; they disturbed him. Yee Chen talked of his business, his palace and the events that had occurred in the city of Mong.

'Duke Cheng died,' he'd say.

'Who killed him?' Zhuang would inquire, out of politeness.

'He got indigestion from shellfish that were not fresh. His end was quick and bizarre. Lately, the poor man had surrounded himself with magicians. He was infatuated with them. You heard of Tso Tse?'

Zhuang was about to tell his father-in-law that magicians' tricks bored him and were vain amusements, but he kept quiet and let him talk while he watched his willow trembling in front of the window; crickets were giving a concert in the tree.

'Tso Tse really had an evil influence,' Yee Chen went on. 'Our duke met him when he was hosting a feast for his vassals. He had invited soothsayers—well-known magicians. When the cook warned him there wouldn't be fish from the river, Tso Tse intervened in his low voice: 'Yes, there will be fish.' He asked for a copper pot, filled it with water and then, with a hook at the end of a bamboo line, out of the pot he fished a bass of a kind much appreciated in Xinjiang. He repeated this a few more times and soon there was enough fish for a hundred guests. Then he poured the water from his pot into the goblets held out to him: it turned into wine, and everyone drank.'

'That's a fascinating fable indeed, Noble Yee Chen.'

'I was there, I saw it with my own eyes, and tasted the fish and the wine! From that miraculous day on, Tso Tse became the privileged adviser to that unfortunate duke.'

'He could have stopped the duke from eating rotten shellfish.'

'I hadn't thought of that, but yes, that's true. I see your reasoning is as sharp as it was before, Zhuang. Tell me, since the duke is dead, don't you want to come back to Mong? I may still need your advice.'

'In the city? I feel too unhappy there.'

'Are you afraid of running into your half-brothers who think you're dead? You could change your name and your appearance and move into my palace.'

'Returning to Mong would be going backwards. And then what? Walking down the same streets, run into the same faces? Live in your house as a recluse? Rush over when you need me?'

'The Pavilion is my house, too.'

'I didn't ask for anything. True, reality is whatever happens, but I endured too much for the sake of propriety. Today, let me choose my own way.'

Zhuang had not entirely rid himself of his education. He still practiced the art of archery as old Confucius taught, to strengthen his powers of attention. Confucius used to repeat that one must never stop perfecting oneself, and that if the arrow missed its target, the archer should only blame himself. Each year, Zhuang participated in an archery contest in the large room of the district school. There, he rubbed shoulders with other competitors from the region; music regulated their gestures and they shot in rhythm side by side. He returned from the contest with his mind refreshed. He also used this art to hunt birds. The moving target enabled him to test his skill at anticipating a trajectory. So one day, in the middle of the Year of the Fire Dog, shortly after he turned forty, Zhuang took his bow and went out to hunt in the park of Tiao Ling.

Zhuang was walking along with his bow in his hand, watching for a bird he imagined himself plucking and roasting on a spit over a woodfire flavoured with thyme. Suddenly, he sensed a flapping of wings behind him and just had the time to duck: a giant magpie grazed his temple and flew up to a branch at the edge of a chestnut grove. 'What a silly animal!' Zhuang said to himself. 'That magpie has large wings but doesn't know how to fly! What's the use of its big eyes if it's not able to avoid an obstacle?' He folded his brown robe and walked towards the little wood. He took an arrow out of the quiver on his shoulder and aimed at the motionless bird. That magpie was oblivious to him or his arrow: it seemed engrossed by one specific sight. Zhuang squinted and spotted a cicada resting in the shade between two blades of grass. Close by, a soft-green praying mantis was ready to jump on the cicada and lunch on it. Zhuang realized that these animals thought only of their prey and ignored the danger that could appear at any moment. They were prisoners of their appetite, oblivious to anything else. Just then he heard the thundering voice of a forester who mistook him for a poacher and came running towards him. He took to his heels and realized that he was just as unaware as the magpie or the mantis. That day, Zhuang acquired a certainty: violence spared no one, and death was always on the prowl. How could one flee from this reality? We are not immortal. For the next three days, he shut himself away in his tower at the Pavilion of the Green Torrent.

CHAPTER TWENTY

The Righteous Robber

Zhuang had wondered at length about the revelation in the park of Tiao Ling. Of whom, or of what, were we the prey? Vultures were turning ceaselessly over our heads, in wait for us to lower our guard. He had laughed at that magpie concentrating on the insect it was going to swallow, but he himself was like that bird; the forester who'd pursued him was proof of that. No sooner had he emerged from seclusion, sure of being on earth as a mere passenger among the others, than he visited the village of Tong Ha to seek the comfort of the fishermen's presence. Seeing the first huts, he thought they had all decided to meet there by that spot on the Yellow River but, as he got nearer, he saw them piling their families onto the boats with their possessions—stools, rolled-up nets, large pots. He had admired the slow precision of these people's movements, but now their gestures seemed erratic, given over to panic. He approached one of the villagers he knew well. The man was almost mute; his usual beatific smile had changed into a frozen grin. He was also moving out.

'What's going on?' Zhuang asked.

'Look at the river.'

Zhuang saw hacked-up bodies rolling in the waters. Some clumped together to form islands bristling with arms and legs already stiffened by death. A gutted baby drifted past. His mother followed in the current with her uncoiled intestines floating around her.

'Why those corpses floating in the river?'

'Che the Brigand is in our region. He's looting, killing, ransacking the whole area. We're leaving.'

'Where is he?'

'Some peasants told us he set up camp in the Valley of the Four Winds.'

'I'm going there.'

'To put an end to his lust for carnage by playing your flute?'

'I'll go to him and find the right words. '

'The words! He couldn't care less about your words!'

'I don't care about words either, but they can be used to persuade.'

'What will you tell him?'

'I will tell him the story of the owl and the cuckoo.'

'What's that?'

'The owl had decided to leave the country he'd always lived in. "People here are afraid of my hoots," said the owl. The cuckoo answered that people elsewhere wouldn't like it either, "You would do better to change your hoot."'

The fisherman shrugged and pressed his kids to get into the overloaded boat. Zhuang made haste to return to the Pavilion of the Green Torrent, and asked for his quadriga.

It was night when Zhuang arrived at the pass that led to the valley. The village he had so often crossed was destroyed, the dried mud walls of the houses now rubble. A few big fellows wearing wolfskin and stolen helmets were piling up the dead like logs. When Zhuang stepped down from his cart, the looters surrounded him and threatened him with their swords and spears. A weasel-faced ruffian began to cut the harness of Zhuang's carriage:

'Hey!' Zhuang said, 'Leave my horses alone!'

'Shut up, foreigner!' said a colossus wearing a belt with amulets and knives hanging from it.

'I'm foreign, yes, especially to your practices.'

'What you want?'

'I've heard of the lofty sentiments of your general. I've come to see him.'

'He know you?'

'Go tell him Zhuang Zhou is asking him for an audience.'

'You look pretty sure of yourself . . .'

'I am.'

Surprised by Zhuang's firm tone and lack of fear, two ruffians were sent to the tent of Che the Brigand. In a corner, sitting on a half-charred beam, a fat hairy man wearing a tiger-tooth necklace was opening the bellies of corpses with his war dagger and then other men flung them on a pile. He was taking out bleeding livers with his two red hands and dropping them into a big wooden basin.

'What you lookin' at me for?' asked the butcher, as he kept on with his task.

'What are you going to do with those livers?'

'Ah, that's for our general, he loves to eat. We cook him little pâtés of minced human livers, peasant livers are the most tasty cause those damn earth-scrapers just stuff themselves with grass!'

The two emissaries came running back from the tent of General Che. Astonished by his leniency towards a stranger, they announced that Zhuang was expected.

A hundred thousand men were camping in the valley. They had chopped down most of the trees and used them to build huts and enclosures for the herds of water buffalos they had requisitioned. They had set up bivouacs here and there on the scorched grass. They were roasting pieces of meat over the fires and heating strange broths in cauldrons. The wavering light of torches wedged in the ground illuminated the valley. Guarded by a hundred armed mercenaries, General Che's tent was planted in the midst of the noisy troops who were drinking, guzzling food and groping young slave girls who'd been forced out of villas and towns and spared, to satisfy the men.

Che was lying on a rush mat. He sat up when Zhuang entered. The tent was a jumble of looted stuff. Part of his booty was piled up in a mess: varnished pieces of furniture, sacks of ingots, chests stuffed with jewels. Che did not look like the other bandits. He had stood up—a tall man with clear eyes and a tunic sewn with golden plaques:

'Zhuang! If you hadn't given your name, I wouldn't have recognized you.'

'Because we know each other?'

'We used to, a long time ago, when we were fifteen.'

'Che . . . the boy I counted quail with in the palace kitchens?'

'And the one who fled from Mong with you.'

'I wouldn't have recognized you either.'

They sat down on square, black lacquer armchairs and Che had wine brought in. As they drank and drank again, they talked. Zhuang explained to his childhood friend that he had lost sight of him in Linzi where they had taken refuge.

'I entered the Association of Mount Hua very quickly, to study and think,' Zhuang said.

'As for me . . . my school was the dives of Linzi.'

'You could have joined me. You would have been considered as a man of letters . . . '

'You mean as a poor man of letters? No thanks! I chose the hoodlums. They lived better, and with more intensity. I quickly became the leader of a band of robbers because I could write and I'd read the classics. See, that did help me around that ignorant bunch! I led a band, then a troop, and now an army of brave devils that strikes fear into the regions I go through.'

'That's odd, Che, coming from a boy who was made to recite whole lines of Confucius just like me.'

'Don't even talk about that!'

That reminder of the past annoyed Che the Brigand.

He emptied a new cup in one gulp and offered little liver pâtés to Zhuang, which he refused. Che swallowed three at a time and began walking in circles. He was losing his temper:

'Confucius! That faker with a crushed prime rib around his waist! He never ploughed for what he ate, never weaved his clothes, and yet he gave people lessons! He misled princes but the princes rebelled against him. He was a criminal driven out of everywhere he went!'

'Like you.'

'No, Zhuang. I'm the one who drives people out.'

'Instead of sacking cities, you never thought of settling down in any of them?'

'Never!'

'And yet, you have virtues. You are tall and slender, both young and old like you, your voice is mellifluous. You can make decisions, guide people and lead them. You are courageous. You could found a city and settle there with a hundred thousand families . . .'

'Zhuang, I have no need of your praise. You're suggesting I should govern a city? How long would I stay there? You can never sleep in peace nowadays. They say that in the past people didn't kill each other, that they were supremely virtuous, but that Yellow Emperor whose praises are so loudly sung spread a sea of blood over the plain of Zhuolu! King Yao was a bad father. Their successors brought tyranny and confusion. How many murdered sovereigns were exposed in brine at the eastern gate of their city? They were all revered, and passing time has erased their misdeeds and embellished their lives, but I find them shameful!'

'Because they gave up their natural feelings for the lure of gain.'

'Your sages are no better off, Zhuang. Look how they ended up. Shentu's prince didn't listen to him, so he tied a heavy stone around his neck and jumped into a river where the fish devoured him. That man, wise though he claimed to be, sought only fame. And died of it. As for me, I want nothing.'

'Yes, you do—gold.'

'Not even that. My loot goes first to my men.'

'You are the most virtuous of men,' Zhuang said in an amused tone.

'What kind of nonsense are you spouting there?'

'You possess four of the essential virtues, Che, my friend—bravery, sincerity, loyalty and patience.'

'I'll leave that accounting to you. Where do our lives lead us? Take away old age, mourning, sorrows and misfortunes—how much time do we have left for a hearty laugh?'

Zhuang was listening to his friend rapturously. He envied his vitality. Che had a thousand reasons to get angry at his rigid, closed education and to blame Confucius, who symbolized it. Confucius, that schoolteacher who remained a schoolteacher till he died; he held on to a practical, limited vision of life; for him, problems were confined to the horizon of a classroom. He never wanted to break down walls, take off, step outside his own will and into the open air to confront life. After the many adventures he hadn't desired, did that peaceful man take advantage of them and open up? No. On the contrary, he locked himself into his books. He wore out whatever health he had left, to read the *Book of Transformations,* again and again. He regretted not knowing it by heart. Then, at the very end, to express his philosophy of the history of mankind, he exhausted himself in refining a compilation, *Annals of the State of Lu.* So he perished in his books and scholars worshipped him for that very reason. But he never strove to stretch his nature to the limit. Zhuang reproached him for not going far enough, as if he had fallen asleep along the way or lacked courage, or imagination, or never knew how to dream. And he repeated to himself that he, Zhuang, would surpass the old master and his dead books.

Che was nibbling a little liver pâté.

'Sure you don't want any? You were more curious when we pretended to be at work in the kitchens of that stupid, old duke. It's delicious, I can assure you.'

Zhuang accepted, tasted one of the human liver pâtés and thoroughly enjoyed it.

They talked all night. Finally, Zhuang asked his friend for a favour: 'Here, the region is poor, what can you get from it? You need fishing nets? You want to steal the peasants' crude wooden instruments? I live here, in this region, and I know what I'm talking about. Spare the banks of the Yellow River. Go add to your loot further north, where the lands are rich.'

In the name of their former complicity, Che agreed to grant peace to the region and leave at the next moon with his hundred thousand rascals. They said goodbye at daybreak. Che had his old companion escorted to the entrance of the pass that opened into the valley, where Zhuang saw his four horses had been stolen. So much the worse for him. He picked up a large, straight branch and made himself a walking stick. Then he climbed up by the path alongside the rocks to the platform from where he loved to listen to the wind. The landscape he saw from up there when the sun rose distressed him. He contemplated the destruction of his forest, the fallen trees, cut or broken, the smoke from the bivouacs, Che's men stirring restlessly around like fleas, not quite awakened yet from their night of drinking. No sound rose up but a diffused hubbub. He set off, yawning, on a path that went around the hills.

CHAPTER TWENTY-ONE

An Encounter with a Skull

After walking for four hours, Zhuang sat down by the side of the path in the shade of a leafy tree. He stretched out and propped up the nape of his neck on a large stone. This pillow was white, smooth and soft, but so light that when he put his head on it, it rolled down the slope. He followed along, picked it up from the ground and just as he turned it around, he realized it was a skull, intact and polished by many rains. He spoke to it ceremoniously:

'Pardon me, O Noble Deceased, I took you for a large stone.'

Zhuang looked around to see if he could locate the rest of the skeleton and wondered how the head had ended up against the trunk of a lone mulberry tree. No tibia, no femur to be seen in the whole countryside. How did this man die? Of hunger? thirst? illness? old age? Why had he been abandoned in nature like an animal? Had his head been cut off with an axe? Was he dishonest, unlucky? Did he die in a war? This bodiless head intrigued Zhuang. When did this man breathe his last? A year ago, ten years, a century? The skull shone in the sun. Zhuang put it back under his tree and rested his head on it to sleep, for he had enough of his unanswered questions, and he'd been sleepy for hours. He no longer tried to resist and let himself be taken over by fatigue, which was stronger than his vain curiosity.

He fell asleep under the mulberry tree.

The skull appeared to him in a dream and wanted to explain itself:

'My poor Zhuang, you are too curious. What you imagined about me was pointless. I died—that's the only fact that matters. At what age? Pfff . . . They say tortoises live a thousand years. Good for them, but that, too, is pure conjecture. What good does it do them to live so long? To climb trees? Sail on lotus leaves? To grasp the language of men and hide to protect themselves from it? Where I'm from, near the Huai River, children's beds are propped up with tortoises. Generations of children have slept in them and then one day, when the children disappear, the bed is moved out but the tortoises are still alive. They had nothing to eat or drink for fifty years, and yet they survived . . .'

'I see. You were a hermit and you wanted to live on your breath alone, like the tortoises.'

'I never had that pretention. I had a trade, I forgot which one . . . Doesn't matter, since I'm dead.'

'Why tell me all this?'

'To instruct you.'

'And . . . ?'

'You found me, showed interest in me. When I come upon a human being who's not too stupid, I feel like talking to him. Would you like me to tell you about death?'

'Sure.'

'A short while ago, you brought up the servitudes the living are subjected to, but all that no longer exists for me. I am dead, you fool, OK? I've reached serenity. In death, there is no more work, no more seasons, no princes or beggars. Nothing above, nothing below.'

'That is pleasant indeed . . .'

'I live detached from the ups and downs of the world and I know supreme joy. No prince, however powerful he may be, can reach such joy. I leave him to his golden possessions, to his schemes, his lies, his little tricks and little gratifications! As for me, I have Heaven and Earth in all their duration.'

'All right, I understand you, O Happy Nameless One, but if I offered you to regain your body of flesh and blood through magic, and return you to your family, your parents, your wives, your children and your friends, what would you say?'

'You're forgetting my barnyard.'

'Stop the mockery . . .'

'Fool! Triple fool! You want to burden me with illnesses and decrepitude by giving me back my body? My family inherited my land a long time ago. You really think they'd have a great desire to see me again? You want me to give up endless joy and be subjected again to the pains and misfortunes of life on earth?'

CHAPTER TWENTY-TWO

Mortal Fevers

At the Pavilion of the Green Torrent, Zhuang resumed his observations of the animal world. Just after the monsoon, when side roads had turned into mud, he focused his attention on the behaviour of a tribe of red ants. They had stopped short at the edge of a rut and were feeling out the water with their feet. One of them slipped, fell into the puddle, struggled to get out, and drowned. They wanted to cross over, but how? Then Zhuang saw that each ant loaded a larva under its belly and dived in. The larvae fastened under their belly were lighter, they floated better and served as tiny boats for them. Having crossed to the other side, the insects laid down the larvae in the sun to dry, set out once more on their procession and disappeared into the grass. Zhuang reflected that the Chinese used their children for their own convenience, the way the ants used their larvae: the boys' purpose was to prolong the name of the family line, and the girls', to breed with the same goal. Zhuang found that custom quite outmoded. It gave people the impression of surviving vicariously underground, nibbled by maggots. People reassured themselves however they could, by inventing traditions, by hanging the names of the departed on their family altars.

Zhuang had two sons by Chao Yun, still very young, but he'd never been truly interested in them. He knew now that the immortality predicted by the sorcerers did not exist. The children lived in the hands of the serving-women who nurtured them the way Zhuang had been nurtured in his father's harem. When they reached the age of one, there was a ritual ceremony by the banks of the Yellow River. The children, each in turn, had been shut in a room in front of an assortment of plates and bowls filled with hazelnuts, paintbrushes, coins and needles. From what they grabbed first, one could tell what their calling would be. The elder rushed over to the nuts and broke them open by knocking them on the floor; they guessed he would be a belly. The youngest immediately grabbed a brush, sucked on it, and pretended to trace arabesques—a career as a palace scribe was predicted for him. Standing a little apart, Zhuang let them prophesize because after all, one had to abide by local customs. Those miniature men, he thought, would grow up to become whatever they could.

Ever since he had been able to dissuade Che the Brigand by the sole strength of his conviction, Zhuang was thought to be a great master at the fishermen's village. Because of their veneration, he went there less frequently so as not to be subjected to their excessive politeness. One day, however, a little boy who helped his father on the Yellow River came running to the Pavilion. He asked for Master Zhuang, who then came down from the tower where he'd been recording his latest observations on chimpanzees and how they cured themselves by chewing on leaves they selected. The boy nervously explained they needed his guidance at the village. Zhuang followed him and inquired further on the way but in vain.

Assembled before the first houses of Tong Ha, the crowd of villagers opened before Zhuang. At one threshold, young men in leather masks representing wild animals were dancing like devils. A tireless tambourine player, dripping with sweat, gave the rhythm to this furious choreography. Zhuang drew nearer. Inside the house he saw a dying man with a grey complexion lying on a reed mat, shaken by spasms. In front of him, the sorcerer was holding a rooster with its legs bound, shaking it so hard he was ripping out its feathers; he was capturing the illness and transferring it to the bird.

Zhuang joined a group of women wearing straw hats squatting against a low wall and keening. Between two sobs and three sniffs, they wailed:

'It's the fever, Master! The fever's coming down on us!'

'But we didn't do anything bad!'

'The fevers are going to eat up the village!'

'Do something, Master Zhuang!'

Zhuang saw another fisherman further on, stretched out on the riverside, trembling in every limb; he was gaping like a fish on the sand. When he walked past prostrate villagers with empty eyes and shaking violently, Zhuang realized an epidemic was spreading fast despite the magical screeching of the shaman with the chicken. And the Pavilion of the Green Torrent would not remain immune from this scourge.

While the epidemic struck, the doctors and sorcerers, out of precaution, sought refuge in a wing of the Pavilion. By using their magical tricks, they tried to stop the illness from entering the gate and the thick barrier of laurels that closed off the domain. They bustled about with an inspired look on their faces, some consulting their oracles, others preparing decoctions. Day and night, wood was thrown on the pyres burning in the garden to repel miasmas. From then on, everyone appeared suspect. They watched for redness or bags under the eyes to spot malignant attacks of the fever. If a gardener's complexion was on the grey side (in reality because the situation was provoking insomnia), the others would push him away and refuse to share the servants' dormitory with him. The nervousness of a cook's helper, the fatigue of one of the serving-women—all those negative signs fed into their fear.

The soothsayers squabbled about their predictions. Zhuang felt a little sorry for those phony scientists; he sometimes enjoyed their debates but never intervened. One of these charlatans consulted the *Book of Transformations*, which Confucius himself had commented upon in the past. Zhuang examined his way of interpreting the hexagrams he composed: he would align the dried-up stems of milfoy, whole or broken, chosen at random, and when some of them turned to face the opposite piece, it would be possible to read from one symbol to another by modifying the design.

'You see,' the soothsayer would say, 'Those six little sticks represent thunder in the wind, but when the sixth changes, it means the orphan has seen a chariot full of demons . . .'

'Yes, and?'

'Whole and broken stems represent the world in movement.'

'Yes, and?'

'Look at the new hexagram—our fears must be transformed into a spectacle.'

'Let's try not to play any part in it.'

Unfortunately for Zhuang, he did have a central role to play in the spectacle of the epidemic. Two doctors and a few serving-women, who were wringing their hands, came to get him and bring him to Chao Yun's bedside. She was lying on multiple embroidered cushions, pale, the skin of her face almost translucent, her body rattled by fits of trembling that came and went like waves. Zhuang knelt next to her without a word, his eyes clouded with tears. He placed a little mirror in front of her lips. The mirror should be dulled by her breath, but it remained clear. Chao Yun was not breathing.

'That's impossible!' Zhuang said. 'I left her just a little while ago.'

He picked her up in his arms and hugged her hard before setting her down on her bed again. Her hair was tied into a bun; he took out the mulberry-wood pin that held it up, undid it, arranged her long black hair around her, and let out an endless cry that silenced the birds outside.

At the start of the epidemic the month before, Chao Yun had sent her children to her father's palace in Mong to keep them safe. And now Yee Chen was arriving at the Pavilion of the Green Torrent at the moment his daughter had just died. He heard the news as he got out of his palanquin. Informed of the illness that was plaguing the southern region of the Red River, he was wearing a protective mask, as were the two hundred horsemen in his troupe. The able-bodied servants prostrated themselves before him, nose to the ground, moaning. He heard a furious din coming from the Pavilion on piles built in the middle of the artificial lake. The noise angered him and he ordered a boat to go inspect the source of the racket. There he found Zhuang sitting cross-legged, banging on the bottom of an earthenware jar, bawling out a drinking song. Yee Chen was dumbfounded. Zhuang kept singing his lungs out.

'Zhuang, are you out of your mind? You've been drinking!'

'Not a drop, Noble Father,' Zhuang replied in a gentle voice.

'What's the point of this comedy?'

'What's the point of this malady?'

He started to sing again but so out of tune that Yee Chen couldn't stand it. He bellowed insults to Zhuang:

'You useless wretch! You don't even respect the death of the mother of your children!'

'She's actually lucky,' Zhuang said as he pushed away the jar he was beating on like a drum.

'You insolent pup!'

'One day before her life, where was Chao Yun? Where is she one day after her life? She's in the same place she was in before she was born. She came from a breeze, a breath, she took shape and was transformed with the passing of the seasons. She disappeared before reaching her autumn. She belongs to Heaven and Earth.'

Yee Chen returned to Mong with his daughter's coffin and the cohort of servants; the useless soothsayers and doctors took advantage of the situation to clear out. Zhuang was alone. In a few days, the flowers withered, weeds and nettles grew at the edge of the lake where dead fish now drifted. In the abandoned buildings of the Pavilion, Zhuang picked up some loaves of cornbread and stuffed them into his canvas bag. In Chao Yun's quarters he spread out the tunics she would no longer wear, to set them in the depths of his memory for the last time. He hesitated to carry with him the Goddess of Mercy she resembled, but in the end the white jade statuette found its place in the bag slung over his shoulder along with the loaves. He left his precious research on animals to the mice and shrews, and set out on the road north. He needed nothing else.

CHAPTER TWENTY-THREE

Zhuang the Angry Prophet

For a long time, Zhuang walked along the Yellow River, which he later crossed in a ferry, a kind of long bamboo raft full of peasants and long-haired black pigs at whose hams he looked with hungry eyes. On the other side, he went deep into the brush. 'Here in Wei, no one knows me, I'm anonymous and free of all attachments.'

Exhausted by hours in the sun and sorry he hadn't brought a hat, he plopped himself down on a butte overlooking the meadows. While munching on one of his cornbread loaves, he noticed three followers of Confucius, recognizable by their attire and their square shoes. They were inspecting graves scattered over the field. They picked the most recent one and tried to excavate it with their shovels. One of them stepped aside, sat down and began to consult a scroll he'd taken from a satchel. The coffin was now exhumed and the two others were smashing its lid with iron bars. Zhuang turned to the one who was reading near him:

'Are you desecrators of graves?'

'Not at all!'

'Taking a worm-eaten coffin from its hole and breaking off the lid . . . what do you call that?'

The man answered stiffly, tapping the scrolls of his books pompously:

'We follow the *Book of Rites* of our revered Confucius to the letter.'

His subordinates were now pulling the corpse out. They stripped his shirt off and cast it aside on the grass. The man went on:

'Times are hard, traveller, our perfect mastery of funeral rites is not enough for us.'

'Really?' Zhuang asked, astonished. 'You have a monopoly on funerals and the complicated mourning ceremonies, the gestures, the chants . . .'

One of the grave robbers stood up, sweating.

The man with the book called out to him:

'Are you done?'

'Almost . . .'

'Keep going! Confucius said: "When he was alive, this individual never did anything good; dead, he wears a pearl in his mouth!"'

Cheered up by Confucius' text, which could not be wrong, the two diggers worked harder on the corpse. While one held it by the nape of the neck, the other pushed his metal stick between the lips and with a sudden jerk opened his mouth like an oyster; he groped around inside it with his hand.

'We got it!'

'Show us.'

One of the plunderers held the pearl he'd found on the dead man's tongue between two fingers. 'Ah, Confucius!' Zhuang grumbled, 'That's where your phrases lead us!'

He immediately left the three Confucianists who had earned their day's work.

In the heart of a rundown neighbourhood of the village of Hoa Yang, the shoemaker had gone mad. All the villagers kept repeating it and lamenting: the unfortunate man was making shoes for the left foot only. No one could put on a pair of his shoes any more.

As he was hiking, Zhuang happened to walk by the contested workshop. Consultations, raised arms, lamentations, vociferations—tempers were rising. Zhuang stopped to listen to the complaints.

'Are you really interested in our problems?' a villager said to him casting a sidelong glance.

'I'm interested in everything that happens along my way,' Zhuang replied with a smile.

Disarmed by the apparent affability of this stranger, the villager explained their problem and concluded wryly:

'We're farmers, we don't know how to make shoes. How 'bout you, you're a shoemaker?'

'I have learnt how to weave straw sandals.'

The man turned around to the others who were still babbling away and interrupted the discussions:

'Hey! We found a shoemaker to replace that old nut Seng!'

And so it was that Zhuang settled down in Hoa Yang. A committee of neighbours promptly allocated the workshop to him and he set down his bundle there right away. Zhuang liked the idea of becoming a useful craftsman, but the place was filthy. He began by sweeping out the little room which opened onto the street. He even swept the alley, on the side where everyone tossed their garbage; it was bound to attract rats. Zhuang respected the intelligence of rats, their courage and their ruses to obtain food, but he had no desire to share his new roof with them. He made a rapid inventory of his possessions: a stool, a mat, an earthen stove where he would heat up his wine, the semblance of a farmyard, limited to a rooster and two hens that chased each other around the room or went off to peck grain near some farm. Zhuang sat down between two bales of straw and immediately started weaving sandals. He was rapidly accepted. The villagers paid him in kind, and he could soon fill a jar with new wine, which he let fermenting.

Winter came. The ditches were red with dead maple leaves the wind had blown into them. On the other side of the street, a flock of birds were chirruping in a plum tree to keep warm. Most of the time, Zhuang would wrap a marten fur around his body and think of nothing. He heated melted snow to brew tea with the plants he had dried. With the cold, as people didn't walk through the slush in straw sandals, work was getting scarce, but the villagers of Hoa Yang coddled him to keep him among them. They even offered him a skinned rabbit.

Once the good weather returned, Zhuang resumed weaving straw. He worked with relentless energy. He'd had the time to change his mind and was now protecting a family of rats that had taken shelter from the cold in his shop. They presented him with their latest litter of baby rats. Zhuang found them agile and resourceful and so he spent his free time studying the dozen or so sounds that made up their language. One day, that family scurried under rags in the adjacent alley; an unusual troop of two hundred wagons was advancing at a walk before Zhuang's workshop. The man with feathers in his cap who held the reins of one of the last wagons, stopped and got down from his box with yellow dragons painted on it to look Zhuang in the face.

'Upon my word! Could I be mistaken? It looks like Master Zhuang in that patched-up tunic! Zhuang-the-Rampart-Against-Brigands, Zhuang the hero sung all over the land south of the Yellow River! What are you doing here, cooked by the sun, in this wretched shop?'

'I make straw sandals.'

Zhuang had recognized that braggart, Cao Chang, against whom he had competed several times in the cantonal archery contests. He always let Cao Chang win and then watched him strut around. The fellow enjoyed defeating others; to him the game meant competition only. Those occasions had made Zhuang realize that the spirit of competition was the source of most of our woes, as it meant a strong will to crush others. He raised his eyes scornfully to that peacock Cao Chang, who was glorifying his own exploits:

'Me, I wouldn't sink so low as to weave straw to make a living. Sovereigns recognize my merits and they reward me. I'm back from Qin and well . . . the young king there appreciated me so much he offered me more than a hundred wagons!'

Zhuang looked his former archery comrade up and down.

'Tell me, wise guy, your king of Qin—what does he do when he gets ill?'

'He probably calls his doctor.'

'Yes. He pays whoever extracts a boil for him with a wagon. The one who sucks his haemorrhoids gets six wagons. And so on—the lower the task, the better the retribution.'

'So?'

'So? For that wonderful gift of a hundred wagons, you must have licked your king's ass, at the very least!'

'I won't allow you to . . .'

'Get out of here, you damn fool! Go lick other asses! There's plenty to do. I predict a fine future for you. Me, I'd rather weave sandals, it's nobler.'

People in the neighbourhood saw Cao Chang climb back onto his wagon. He looked furious and whipped his horses angrily. They felt nothing good could come of this for their village and for themselves, who had chosen a shoemaker with a ready tongue. Zhuang continued to weave sandals calmly, as if nothing had happened. A large circle of villagers gathered around him, and one of them coughed to attract his attention:

'You shouldn't have, Zhuang . . .'

'What?'

'You insulted a high dignitary of Song.'

'Certainly. That strutting moron deserved it . . .'

'He's gonna want revenge,' the wheelwright said.

'Him? Don't worry. That pretentious whippersnapper's only power is his ability to crawl before princes. You really think he'll tell the court how I treated him? He would make a fool of himself.'

'You speak of the Duke of Song's court as if you knew it . . .'

'I did know it in the past,' Zhuang smiled, 'But I'm sure it's the same now—an assembly frozen in its rituals in the midst of a changing world.'

'Who are you, Zhuang?'

'Don't worry, my friends, I am Zhuang the Shoemaker.'

The villagers returned to their occupations, but one of them confided to the others in a low voice: 'That's true, we don't know who Zhuang is, we don't even know where he's from . . .'

Indeed, they were not aware that Zhuang had been on an embassy to Qin in the past. Their shoemaker remained quiet about his life. Yet he remembered every detail of his encounter with Shang Yang, that disarmingly vain prince, who later died. Soon after King Hiao's death, his son condemned Shang Yang, accusing him of rebellion; he wanted to have him arrested. Warned of the fate awaiting him, Shang fled. He sought refuge at an inn on the border for one night, but had to identify himself: 'I'm a victim of my own laws.' he sighed. He then fled to Wei where he was refused asylum because of his past treachery and the invasion of that country he himself had ordered. So he shut himself in his fiefdom and raised troops of his own. After some time, he was crushed and killed. The new king of Qin had his corpse drawn and quartered, and executed his family. Prince Shang's cruelty had finally turned against him.

Cao Chang-the-Braggart told no one how Zhuang had chastised him, but to revenge himself, he talked about him and claimed he'd seen him hiding in a village of Wei, disguised as a shoemaker. The rumour spread through Song. Hardly a year passed when a counsellor of the Duke of Song turned up in the village of Hoa Yang with a magnificent retinue escorted by lancers in ceremonial dress.

'Where is Master Zhuang?' the counsellor asked the first peasants he met.

'We don't know,' they said, before shutting themselves in their houses.

When he wanted Zhuang's address, faces would close up or turn away. He finally found him on the banks of the river very close from town. He was sitting on the embankment between two clumps of reeds, fishing.

'Are you Master Zhuang?'

'Yes, my fine prince. How did you recognize me?'

'You don't look like the peasants around here.'

'Yet I try my best to blend into the landscape.'

'And I, Master Zhuang, have come to offer you another landscape that will suit you better.'

'Go ahead, tell me but not too loud or you'll scare my fishes.'

'The Duke of Song wants you near him.'

'I don't know him.'

'But he knows you by reputation.'

'Hup!'

Zhuang had brought up a silvery fish from the water and it was wiggling around at the end of his string. He unhooked it and threw it into a bucket.

'Master Zhuang, our duke thinks you would be very useful at the palace.'

'To put a finishing touch on the decoration? No thanks! I knew your palace all too well. I even saw a big fish with fat lips and eyes round as buttons swimming in a tiny basin there. It hardly had room to turn around, once to the right, once to the left, and it was bored, hugely bored. It would turn and bump into a wall. The people of the palace laughed at its sight, such big creature in that little cube. It only had a decorative function. You want me to be like that fish? Go back where you came from, sir, and let me yawn to my heart's content.'

He sank his line back into the river.

The villagers disapproved of Zhuang's behaviour. They brought him fewer gifts, spent less time chatting with him but didn't dare to say to his face what was bothering them. Zhuang understood that they feared reprisals from the prince because of his sharp tongue, in other words, his forthrightness. These good people must be thinking he was an important person who had fallen out of grace with the Prince and who sent emissaries of the court packing, a court where he must have held an important position. Zhuang couldn't stand the cowardly villagers of Hoa Yang any longer. He looked around, stuffed some biscuits into his canvas sack, added a bowl and a dish, a goatskin flask and the white jade statuette that reminded him of Chao Yun. He went out into the street, leaning on his walking stick. The wheelwright was passing by and looked surprised to see the shoemaker desert his workshop in the middle of the day. Before he could even open his mouth, Zhuang called out:

'You yellow-bellied cowards! I'll leave you to your cowardice. Besides, you were born with it. I have nothing more to learn from you. When I'm far away , you'll feel reassured.'

'But Zhuang, we won't have a shoemaker any more!'

'You should have thought of that sooner. You have to deserve a shoemaker.'

Zhuang turned his back on him and took the road to the mountains. 'Life is divided into seasons,' he said to himself, 'And I'm changing seasons once again.'

A tall, thin, bearded man who had been camping under the plum tree for a few days also picked up his bag and followed him at a distance.

CHAPTER TWENTY-FOUR

The First Disciple

Zhuang didn't notice the walker following him from afar because he never looked behind him. But he could not avoid seeing the family of rats he'd saved from the cold trotting along at his pace. A family? No, a horde. There were now over a hundred of them since a female rat brings twelve baby rats into the world every two months, and in the first litter of that winter, the two young females gave birth in their turn to a dozen babies. Zhuang leaned pensively on his stick. 'Ah, my friends,' he said to them, 'Find a safe place where you can live and grow, but for pity's sake, stop following me!' The oldest rat, the one he'd welcomed into his shop when it was freezing outside, stood up on his hind legs and squealed. 'These rats have a great advantage over men,' Zhuang said to himself. 'They don't think, they know life by instinct. They're grateful, which moves them further away from men but nearer to Heaven.' He kept walking and so did the tribe, on the side of the dusty road that went up towards the mountains.

At night, Zhuang stopped near a clear stream, scooped up water in his bowl to refresh himself. It was in the foothills of the Celestial

Terrace Mountains. He picked a handful of red berries and saw a hare running between the pines and the junipers. He sat down on a flat stone and fumbled around in his bag to restore himself. Suddenly, the rats scattered away. There must be danger.

The danger they sensed was not threatening. The skinny boy who had tailed Zhuang since the village plum tree was now standing in front of him. He had climbed a steep path and was catching his breath.

'Master Zhuang . . .'

'What ill wind brings you here? How do you know who I am and where I was?'

'I come from Mong. Over there, everyone's talking of your exploit and telling how you were able to divert Che the Brigand away from the banks of the Yellow River.'

'People always tell stories about what they haven't seen or experienced.'

'Baron Cao Chang affirmed you'd become a shoemaker in a village of Wei and he mentioned the name of the village where you were working. All I had to do was take to the road.'

'Why?'

'When you were the Supervisor of Lacquers, I was six. I used to bring you crabs.'

'Oh yes! They were delicious.'

'My father called me Number Six but today I invented a name for myself. I am called Tse Lu.'

'Good for you.'

'I rent out my arms for all kinds of jobs. Above all, I know how to garden. I thought that could be useful to you . . .'

'I know how to garden, too, my boy. You still haven't told me the real reason that brought you before me today.'

'One day, you told me to look at a tree and forget its name. At the time, I didn't understand, but I thought of it often before I realized what you meant.'

'What did you realize?'

'That the name is not the thing.'

'Exactly, the name does not have a body, you can't touch it, it has no reality, it's fluctuating and arbitrary, it changes from one region to another. But the thing stays the same. Does this tree give shade? Is its trunk smooth or rough? You have to touch its bark, it's the only conversation you can have with what lives on this earth. Nature is the strongest. Look at the tender grass, bright green, growing on ruins and covering them up. Grass lifts stones, cracks them and goes through them towards the light. Nothing can stop it.'

Zhuang was picking up twigs and branches to make a fire in a circle of large stones.

'Let's see what you have in your bag . . .'

There was a chicken, plums, and beans with their leaves still on them. Zhuang grabbed the chicken, put it on his lap, and began plucking off its feathers. Tse Lu started the fire to cook and to give them light and warmth. Night was falling. Coolness and silence settled around them.

'Master . . .'

'Stop breaking our peace with your questions!'

'Master, why are men the way they are?'

'Damned if I know, my boy.'

'Why?'

'I don't have a clue.'

'Can we ever know anything?'

'I don't know, I said! Just skewer this fowl on the branch you're holding. And, by the way, how did you come upon this chicken?'

'I bought it at the market with what Mr Li gave me when I laid out his garden.'

'Ah, Mr Li, that old windbag of an official! You must have run into Madame Li the coquette, then . . .'

'No, Master.'

'Too bad. In Hoa Yang, they claim she's the most beautiful woman. At the market they go giddy over her. And drool when she passes by . . .'

'Not you, Master?'

'Beautiful, ugly—they're only conventions, you know. What is beautiful? What is ugly? For whom? For what? Madame Li! Monkeys prefer their females over her, stags prefer their does, and for tigers, she's just a piece of fresh meat. Madame Li! When they see her, birds fly away, fish get terrified and dive to the very bottom of the waters. Who's right? Everyone loves the company of whoever resembles them. People hate those who are different.'

When the skin of the chicken sizzled under the flame, they ate in silence and then lay down on the moss in the now dying light of the fire. Zhuang spoke again:

'A leper gave birth to a child in the dead of night. She anxiously grabbed a candle to shed light on the baby: "I so hope he looks like me!"'

CHAPTER TWENTY-FIVE

The Celestial Terrace Mountains

A terrible commotion awakened them before dawn. As the moon was full, they could see two howling men in a tussle. Rats were hanging on to their coats with their claws and biting their calves with warlike shrieks. Surprised by this hairy, aggressive swarm, the rogues were thrashing about violently this way and that, trying to unhook the jaws of the ravenous little beasts without success. They were gesticulating desperately, dancing in the moonlight like grotesque sorcerers. With a sabre he had probably stolen from a dead officer, one of them was exhausting himself in whirling, useless strokes, cutting into empty air. When a fat grey rat jumped on his wrist and another attempted to slip under his sleeves, the weapon fell into the grass. The swaggering soldier joined his accomplice who was running down the slope and almost crashed to the ground after stumbling on a stone. They were running, with rats hanging on to their clothes, staring at them with their red eyes. Still half-asleep, Zhuang and his new disciple got up and grasped their sticks, but the two intruders were already down the hill.

'Thieves,' Zhuang said.

'They didn't even open our bags . . .'

'Because they didn't have time.'

Next to the ashes from the night before, a swarm of little rats was attacking the carcass of the chicken. When dawn rose, our two friends saw the rogues running over the plain as if they had the demons of hell at their heels. Tse Lu grabbed the sword, saying they would need a cutting tool. Without another word, they gathered their belongings and took to the road again, going higher into the mountains.

They climbed up towards the summits permanently blurred by clouds. The rats didn't follow them, as if they had paid their debt by protecting them from the thieves. When they stopped to rest, they saw monkeys and snakes and a pair of hares hurrying into the bushes. They crossed a dense forest peopled by chattering birds, walked for a long time across a plain of rocks and moss, walked along a clear stream full of fish, and in the evening came to a valley of grass so high that Tse Lu had to carve out a path with the sword he'd taken from the bandits. They reached the source of the stream in a heap of rocks and saw open caves on the side of a cliff. They decided to settle in one of them for the night or longer, when they had finished exploring the surroundings. They had crystal-clear water, always cool, that came out of the ground. It remained to be seen what the nearby forest could offer by way of fruit and meat.

They sat down and ate the plums Tse Lu had brought along. Zhuang filled his flask at the spring. The next day he would weave mats with the lianas that were swinging above a thicket of giant bamboos. Tse Lu asked:

'Master, isn't it dangerous to refuse power as you do?'

'I want to protect myself from that foolishness.'

'Your rejection of power, your lack of personal interest—isn't it what they like?'

'Would they dare track me down here in this mountain, tie me up, chain me, take me back to a boring city to stick me on a throne? I don't think so.'

'That already happened . . .'

'Are you thinking of Prince Seou in the kingdom of Yue?'

'I know nothing of this prince, Master. I was simply alerted by my common sense.'

'Well then, let me tell you—the people of that kingdom had already killed three of their sovereigns. Still, they wanted to install the heir apparent in the royal palace, but sensing the danger, he quickly fled to a cave he thought was inaccessible. The unfortunate prince was wrong—the people of Yue discovered him. They argued with him at the entrance to his cave to persuade him to follow them. He stood firm. The inhabitants of the kingdom lit fires and smoked him out like a fox. He was forced to come out, coughing, teary-eyed, one hand over his nose and mouth. Much against his will, bemoaning his lot, he had to climb into the royal palanquin his subjects had brought. Seou had no desire to be exposed to the fate of most sovereigns—and, in fact, that's why the people wanted him.'

'That's exactly what I was saying, Master!'

'Yes, but I'm not the heir apparent.'

'You have a reputation . . .'

'Alas!'

His disciple reported the conversations he had overheard in the shops of Mong or in the taverns. They related, with a plethora of imaginary details, how Zhuang had diverted the cutthroats of Che the Brigand through his virtue alone. Zhuang was exasperated by the word.

'My virtue! Nonsense! Cat piss! Yes, those brigands don't lack virtue, that's for sure!'

'How's that, Master?'

'Think, you blockhead! They must be clairvoyant to guess where the good people hide all the gold or jade they amass, they must be brave to seize their wealth, to remain alert during a raid, and like the good captains they are, protect their men because of course they have a sense of duty. And in the end, they must carry out, honestly, a fair distribution of the loot. Clairvoyance, bravery, a sense of duty and honesty—aren't those virtues?'

Zhuang was getting carried away all the more as the sky was blue and the clearing peaceful. Now he was speaking of those virtuous people and of those saints who poisoned people's lives.

'Let's eliminate the saints and leave robbers alone! There'll be no more unrest in the world when we're rid of those judgemental lesson-givers. Tell me, what is a scale used for?'

'To weigh things, Master.'

'Yes, but also to fool people. Dishonest merchants know how to rig it, all they think of is duping you about the weight of their merchandise so you pay more than what you really owe. Scales are used to steal and morality covers all kinds of frauds.'

'I guess so . . .'

'Whoever steals a bushel of grain ends up on the gallows and whoever steals a kingdom ends up on the throne. The virtue they preach is actually degrading us. Look at those crowds that rush over as soon as someone tells them a sage is coming to their town. They leave their family, their friends, their possessions, to take refuge in the shadow of a fortune-teller! All our ills come from the fact that men try to know what they can never know instead of turning their attention to what they already know. Those thoughts invented by the sages have laid the world to waste. And then again, what are they, those sages puffed up by pride, if not the docile servants of tyrants?'

While he was conversing, Zhuang seemed to be looking around on the ground for something; suddenly his face lit up, he calmed down and picked up a stone he had just found near the spring.

'Here's my pillow!' he said. 'And now let us sleep, we've jabbered enough. Tomorrow we'll go hunting.'

Tse Lu had kept the pits of the plums they'd just eaten. He planted them in the ground with precise gestures while his Master was falling asleep on his stone, thinking of Wen Tse, that old friend he appreciated so much in the past when he was still young and living in exile. And now he was following the same path, speaking in the same manner, quite naturally. Without realizing it, Zhuang had followed the same course.

The next morning, they made themselves bows out of bamboo as Zhuang had learned to do in the past, during his stay with the toadman. Tse Lu cut out arrows and sharpened them with the blade of his sword, but he had been anxious to ask a question and he finally did.

'Master, I don't really understand why you speak of the sages so severely.'

'Mmm . . .' Zhuang answered as he adjusted the strings of the bows.

'Don't they ever give good advice to those who consult them?'

'Nobody comes to consult them. They only go to them to be subjected to their speeches and their hare-brained ideas. What do you think, for God's sake?'

'People seek consolation . . .'

'They hope to take their minds off things. Distraction is the best way of escaping oneself.'

'Distraction from what, Master?'

'They're afraid of everything—their neighbours, their princes, themselves, life. They need distractions to forget their own short-comings. Fear gives birth to a need for comfort, the need for comfort gives birth to beliefs, beliefs give birth to vanity and vanity gives birth to hatred. A fine result! Those earthly gods to whom they sacrifice a pig are pure inventions! As if the gods loved blood sausage! The sac-rificer is the only one to profit from it. The ninnies applaud and ven-erate profiteers! The gods lead us astray, princes lead us astray, prophets lead us astray, ideas lead us astray . . .'

'Are we to believe in nothing?'

'Of course, if your mind is totally free. Reject the memory that encumbers you, the past, the memories, consider the world with a fresh eye, stripped of those old rags. Memory masks reality. What is known is known, and prevents us from looking at reality with fresh eyes.'

'So what remains, Master? A perpetual present?'

'No.'

'What, then?'

'Emptiness.'

As Tse Lu stood there gaping, Zhuang shook him:

'You don't understand a thing I'm saying, do you? True, if you don't know how to wander, you can't understand me. And yet, you simpleton, if there's no emptiness in a house, how could you walk through it? Breathe, forget and taste the coolness of the morning, which is always new.'

Zhuang explained healthy idleness to his disciple. He showed him how people who work with their hands work themselves to death, how thinkers lose themselves in their artifices until they become anxious and fall ill, how it's better to have no talent or trade so nobody can ask anything from you. We can only watch, Zhuang said, and live restfully, filling our bellies, dancing and sleeping. We must lead our lives like an empty boat drifting with the currents.

With their bows in their hands, they walked downhill, following the trickle of fresh water that turned into a stream, then into a small river running through a plain abounding with game down below. They held back their steps and their breath when they came upon a silver fox hesitating at the water's edge. Thanks to its sense of smell, the animal knew of their presence but seemed reluctant to swim across the river. It turned this way and that, seeking a way out, but was trapped between the men and the water. Then it resolved to face the situation and held itself stiffly on its paws. Tse Lu prepared an arrow but Zhuang held him back.

'Why kill this fox?'

'For our dinner, Master.'

'Fox meat is inedible. Hunters kill it for its fur. Some animals end up in stews, others in clothes. Do you want a silver fox collar?'

'Me? No, not at all.'

'So put down your bow. You see, this fox is as arrogant as a man, it doesn't want to dirty its fur by crossing the river. It would rather face us and get killed than get wet. Help me . . .'

Zhuang pointed to a large branch that had fallen on the grass, probably severed by lightning. They carried it and threw it into the riverbed. Then they backed away. The fox came over to the log and jumped on this improvised bridge. It disappeared into the grass on the other side of the river.

'We'll have to resign ourselves to replacing hunting by gathering, my friend,' said Zhuang. 'What are the fruits over there in the underbrush?'

CHAPTER TWENTY-SIX

At the Village

On another hunt, they pushed further into the mountains and that was when Zhuang and Tse Lu encountered the mountain dwellers. First they heard a sad, melodious song whose words were incomprehensible to them: '*Mwav tas wa le: quan tsi tub nyob ntuj . . .*' They let themselves be guided by the voices, which grew louder as they approached them. After climbing a steep, sandy slope, they came onto a hamlet—three long bamboo houses around a bare meadow where the mountain dwellers were honouring a corpse lying on slats. The women wore many chiselled silver jewels and the men, large black jackets. One of them was wrapping half of a chick and a grain of rice in a red cloth on the dead man's belly. The two visitors sat down in a corner so as not to disturb the unfamiliar ritual, nor that interminable song in an unknown dialect. Tse Lu looked attentively at the buildings that stood out against the forest and the fog-covered mountains. At the end of the ceremony, the mountain dwellers invited the travellers to rest awhile in the chieftain's house and offered them a bowl of warm water. The conversation was short and minimal, all in gestures, and then Zhuang and Tse Lu returned to their grotto with a gift of two chickens.

'Master, their constructions are skilful. We should build cabins before the rainy season, too. I took careful note of how we should go about it . . .'

'Yes . . .'

'Are you listening, Master?'

'Yes . . .'

Zhuang was not listening, but answered yes out of politeness while he continued thinking out loud:

'Those poor mountain dwellers imagine death as a voyage. They put a snack on the belly of the corpse, did you see? Surely the way is long to meet the spirits of the ancestors somewhere or other! Again that human, too-human need to always look for reasons. They don't know, or don't want to believe, that the dead are dead. Fate grants us so many years to live, Tse Lu, so make sure you live life to the fullest, with the smallest possible number of torments. We are limited in a limitless world, we'll pass through this earth as quickly as the shadow of a galloping horse. Oh, my! Hey . . . I know that big rock with a silhouette of a vulture, we're not far from our cave . . . Let's walk faster, night's going to fall . . .'

They built two reed huts that resembled the mountain dwellers' cabins, and a kind of awning to protect the entrance to the main cave, which would serve them as a storehouse. The plum tree was growing but the forest was rich in fruits and they spent most of their time hunting or fishing in the river below. They knew their food had medicinal benefits: Zhuang picked grasses or roots that kept them in good health. To repel mosquitos and snakes they prepared an ointment out of crushed ants as he had seen monkeys do.

With the seeds the mountain people had brought them at the beginning of their encounter, they turned a square of the wild forest into a garden. They harvested squash and cucumbers. They used bamboo for everything: they ate the young shoots, hollowed out the stalks to make flutes, rubbed two pieces together in the morning to start the fire. During the seasons of rain and snow, they shut themselves inside their hut.

Time went by.

Tse Lu would go down to the villages in the valley once a year. There, he traded the utensils they had made and returned to their cabins with salt and wine. One day, he came back up with mules and two companions whom he introduced as wandering scholars. The elder had a thin beard of sparse white hair. He had studied Confucius in the past but realized that his teachings were limited. Then he had venerated Mozi but had exhausted his lessons of austerity; and then Xunzi, who was too categorical:

'I heard about you, Zhuang—you preach idleness.'

'They know of me in the cities?'

'Oh yes, Master,' replied the younger scholar. 'They even claim you are incorruptible.'

'With your permission, we will come live with you,' the elder chimed in, 'So you can show us the path to follow.'

'I have nothing to teach you. Our competence is limited. *We can only observe and describe.*'

CHAPTER TWENTY-SEVEN

The Earth from Above

Tse Lu served as an intendant; Zhuang delegated the ordinary, practical, daily chores to him. That's how he got to take care of the two new arrivals during the Master's nap, and discovered a dizzying quantity of brushes, ink sticks and thin wood tablets strung together in the baggage the mules had been carrying. He made an enclosure for the animals and helped his companions build cabins. After this agitation, they all went back to their own reveries. Later, they constructed a little pavilion on piles, where they could write. On some evenings, Zhuang did the honours: he would prepare dishes the way he had seen them made at the Duke of Song's palace long ago, but he allowed himself to improvise, mixing river carp with tapir legs. The younger of the scholars who was useless at any practical task, was appointed as Watcher of Flies. Zhuang explained to him that flies were as indomitable as hyenas and because they love dirt, excrements, and all kinds of rotten things, put their soiled legs on food; the other one, the respectful and docile scholar, armed with palm leaves drove potential flies away from the stone stove.

Zhuang never made speeches: he even claimed that eloquence should be banished and was not worth silence. But sometimes he responded to the curiosity of his companions.

One day, the oldest scholar expressed his pity for Zhuang when he saw his robe full of holes and his sandals patched up with string.

'So what?' Zhuang said. 'These sandals are for walking, the robe is for dressing, they fulfil their function and they suit me fine.'

'Dressed like that, Master Zhuang, you are the very face of distress!'

'Poverty is not distress, my little friend. You're using the same words the Duke of Wei once used about me!'

Zhuang had answered the duke that monkeys who are used to big trees can jump from branch to branch with great agility, sheltered from arrows, but if they're put in a landscape of bushes or brush, they walk clumsily, trembling, afraid of hunters. That is what happens to the wise man in hostile surroundings; under a bad sovereign he cannot display his knowledge—he's crippled, unsure and fearful. He's in distress.

'Poverty is not distress, I'm telling you! Here in the midst of nature, what's the use of your embroidered robe? You want to compete with the parrots? At that game, they'd beat you hollow.'

'You are right, Master Zhuang,' the scholar sheepishly agreed.

'An embroidered robe! That's fine at the court, or to please the crowd that comes to hear your catchy speeches! Is the crowd always right? A crowd remains at the surface of things and lets itself be guided by its emotions.'

A few afternoons later, while Tse Lu was teaching Watcher of Flies how to light a fire, Zhuang resumed his conversation with the other one, whom he had named Greybeard.

'I was familiar with wealth, you know, I studied it up close and even took advantage of it. But believe me, the spectacle of dignitaries humiliating themselves before the rich, those walking gold ingots, is sickening. Those humiliated men also dream of honours and wealth. Poor buggers! They lose their intelligence and willpower; they neglect the most important thing.'

'Which is . . .?' asked Greybeard.

'Heaven, of course!'

'And yet, Master Zhuang, wealth gives men what they may desire . . .'

'Pfff!'

'Isn't the thirst for power innate? It's part of human nature . . .'

'Pfff! When you are sated with everything, you grow soft, it's as if you were walled in abundance, buried inside of it. How sad! How despicable! Rich or poor, the wise man is always joyful. Our possessions are transient. They come and go. The joy power brings you is a lie. We forget our true nature.'

'What do you mean, Master?'

'I say what I say and nothing more, you sneaky teaser! You always need to find a hidden meaning behind simple facts! Stop thinking! It's harmful to your health and other people's, too.'

Annoyed, Zhuang went to sit on a big rock to warm himself in the sun. A lizard came out of a rock pile, settled down next to him and fell asleep by his side.

By the evening of that same day, Zhuang had not moved from the rock he'd been sitting on. Tse Lu walked quietly over on the moss and ventured a question:

'Master, our companions are afraid of being rebuffed and don't dare question you about their doubts . . .'

'I don't give a hoot about their doubts. All they have to do is raise their eyes like me—here, look at the full moon taking shape even before nightfall.'

'That's just it, you talk about Heaven all the time but they don't understand exactly what you're putting into that word.'

Zhuang stretched out his legs and took a deep breath.

'The water buffalo has four legs, that's Heaven. His nose is pierced by a ring, that's man. Heaven is inside, man is outside. Heaven is innate, what is human is acquired. If you're venerated because you do nothing, that's Heaven's mode of action; being the prisoner of things and acting is man's mode of action . . .'

'Is the action of man necessarily harmful?'

'Man's action? Ha! ha! ha! Calculation and efficiency! Men create machines that create mechanical activities in their turn, and they mechanize their own heart. Goodbye candour, goodbye peace of mind . . .'

'How can one survive far from men?'

'I never said that! Don't let outside circumstances influence you, Tse Lu. We must develop the celestial part of ourselves without neglecting our human part, we cannot restrain one and neglect the other. But the human part must not destroy the celestial.'

And with that, Zhuang went to fill his flask at the stream.

Three springs later, our companions woke to a morning with no birds singing. No sooner were they up, holding their robes with both hands, than they spotted Zhuang in the distance and ran to join him. He was standing motionless at the edge of the rocky mound that looked over the plain. They heard the rumble of a storm and were surprised: it never rained in this season. As they gathered around Zhuang and looked down, they realized where that rumbling was coming from. The echo of a thousand drums was rising to their refuge. A huge army was marching in serried ranks behind banners, through the alfalfa fields lying fallow.

'Wow!' said Watcher of Flies. 'My God, how many can they be?'

'At least three hundred thousand,' Zhuang replied.

After invading the whole kingdom of Wei, the soldiers of Qin were marching south towards Song.

'It's been ages since we've had a war,' Zhuang said cheerfully. 'It didn't seem normal to me.'

'They advance as if they were happy to get killed,' added Tse Lu.

'They are happy indeed. The tribes are in a warlike mood. Those soldiers have a strong sense of superiority, skilfully disguised as necessity by their generals. Each man feels protected by the group, they feel they have roots, and they're not treated like vagrants.'

Zhuang then took on a more learned tone to analyse the situation. If Ts'i, to the east, helps Song to resist, Qin is going to face an army of similar size. And he imagined the encounter, the clash of those two howling masses, the dull sound of the catapults, the whistling bolts of the crossbows, the shock of lances piercing the cuirasses of water-buffalo hide. The cries of fury. The groans of the dying. The bowels slashed out of bellies and trampled by a new wave of attackers.

'You seem to be amused by that vision, Master . . .'

'What a beautiful spectacle!' Zhuang said. Just look at those hyp-notized fowls marching in step behind the turkeys leading them to the slaughterhouse! What a sight!'

'But for what?' lamented Watcher of Flies.

'For very little. To nibble on new territories and new riches. You see, the ugliness of this world lies in thinking that it belongs to us.'

Then Zhuang said something that disconcerted his disciples:

'I wonder if those ugly lice really exist or if they're just populat-ing our nightmares?'

'They look like they do exist, Master. They're moving their legs and wearing their weapons on their backs.'

'At a prince's court, I saw automatons that served guests with drinks, and others, in bronze, that made up an orchestra and played excellent tunes thanks to some machinery made of wires and bellows . . .'

And Master Zhuang told them the story of King Mou, to whom an inventor presented a puppet he was proud of: 'You'll see, My Lord, how it can dance better than a man.' He fiddled with something in the back of his doll and threw it into action. The puppet whirled around, jumped, turned, bent, leapt, multiplied entrechats with its arms rounded, and finally bowed to the company. When the queen wanted to look at this mechanical prodigy up close, the puppet smiled at her and put its hand on her bum. Furious at this naughty mischief, King Mou called his guards to have the inventor executed, but taking hold of the puppet, the inventor opened its thorax and displayed its mechanism. Charmed, filled with wonder, King Mou cried out: 'So the art of man can compete with Creation!' Master

Zhuang concluded, while the shining armies of Qin marched off by the foot of the mountain in perfect order:

'King Mou's automaton resembled a man through its gestures, its moods and its behaviour. Now, aren't there a great many men who resemble automatons?'

CHAPTER TWENTY-EIGHT

'A Disgusting Bunch of Sheep!'

The incessant wars between the Chinese kingdoms drove the most peace-loving, unemployed scholars into exile in the mountains or in the remote wilderness, far from devastation, pillage, rapes, fires and mass executions. A number of these refugees had settled at the edge of Zhuang's village, with cabins added to cabins. New plots of jungle had to be cleared, pointy-leaved bamboo trees had to be trimmed and the cultivated land around the plum trees Tse Lu had planted, which now bore fruit, had to be extended. They also had to build more enclosures for the animals, for some fugitives had arrived with farm animals, and even long-maned horses. Soon there were thirty odd scholars, including two families with wives, concubines and children.

Zhuang refused to assume any authority, but everyone, knowing his worth, stayed away from his den and the paths he took for his walks so as not to bother him. The sound of little kids crying barely broke the customary silence. They lived in an autarky and noticed the armies manoeuvring in the valley only by chance. The sickly odour of putrefying corpses did not reach their noses.

Zhuang sometimes chatted with a few of the scholars and sometimes he could even perceive, in the hotchpotch of their theories, an ounce of wisdom. To the one who claimed to be studying the ancient texts he had saved from destruction by packing them into his pouch, he would say:

'What man does not know exceeds all that he knows. Why encumber yourself with that false knowledge?'

To another one who hoped to fortify his body by splashing around in the icy water of the spring, he would say:

'The length of our existence is nothing compared with the time we do not exist.'

To yet another who proposed to better explore the resources of the forest so they could be exploited, he spoke in a more severe tone:

'Leave gold in the mountains and pearls in the waters!'

When the man named Yang, while busy harvesting peas said how kind the followers of Confucius were, he turned cruel:

'Those sectarians only sow disorder! Their affected kindness is only sentimentalism! Tell me, Yang, why do men who are truly merciful always live in misery? Your charitable people look out for other people's suffering so they can publicly display empathy and show themselves in a good light. If kindness and justice are natural feelings, why are people's lives one long lamentation?'

Zhuang told Yang the story of the two servants. They kept sheep together but the animals had escaped without alarming them. The good servant had seen nothing because he was lost in his books, the bad servant had seen nothing because he was playing dice. Whether you think they're good or bad didn't change the result: the sheep had disappeared. What was the point of excusing one and blaming the other?

Master Zhuang brought his friend, Tse Lu, to the cave where the community stored their provisions, for some wine. They lingered under a large tree. Striped squirrels were greedily nibbling the green berries hanging from the branches. Suddenly, they scampered away and the crow that had driven them off landed victoriously on a branch.

'You see,' Zhuang said, 'That crow thinks it's important because it drove away animals weaker than it is.'

'Maybe it's hungry.'

'No, no, not even, it can't stand those berries. It just wants to show its power, a bit like the state employees in charge of food who stop people from making use of the seeds left in buildings, where they'll sprout . . .'

Then they went to get flasks of wine and realized their reserves were diminishing. Soon they'd have to organize an expedition into the valley to get fresh supplies.

'Can you see a spot on our mountain where grapevines might grow?'

'There's a hillside beyond the forest that seems to have good exposure,' Tse Lu replied.

'Let's try to plant some,' Zhuang decided. 'It's a pain to depend on the peasants down below to get drunk!'

As they were returning to the pavilion to drink their wine and chatter, they walked by the cabin of Siang-the-Goitrous, lost in the ferns.

Siang had his head upside down and his feet up in the air. Leaning on his forearms, he had raised his legs to the sky with a flexibility you didn't know he had, but his face wasn't visible because of the goitre flapping against his nose.

'Come back to us!' said Zhuang, mockingly.

The man fell back on the ground like a dropped parcel.

'What was that strange posture, Mr Siang, and for what purpose?'

'It's an exercise to become immortal, Master.'

'Who invented that stupid nonsense?'

'Chan-the-Leopard, Master.'

'Dunno the guy.'

'He teaches immortality . . .'

'You become immortal if you hold your head upside down?'

'Yes, Master, it's the right path . . .'

'You, stupid idiot!'

Zhuang took a deep breath to calm the anger rising within him. Tse Lu helped Siang-the-Goitrous get up. As soon as he was upright, the man tried to defend the merits of his practice:

'You yourself, Master Zhuang, advised us to exercise our bodies.'

'By imitating a circus acrobat?'

'I thought . . .'

'You thought! You're hanging on to lies. Immortality—what an illusion! You want to live a thousand years? If no one can stop life from appearing, no one can stop it from disappearing.'

Zhuang launched into a very simple, patient explanation that Siang-the-Goitrous, a lover of ready-made phrases, should be able to understand. When Zhuang spoke of the body, he did not reduce it to a heap of viscera, teeth, hands, bones and skin. He saw it as a whole that constitutes us humans and comprises our intuitions, our moods, our ecstasies and our skills. The body is a whole, a combination of fluxes that come together to transform us into a unique being. After this lesson, he turned scathing again and stared into the poor goitrous man's eyes:

'You triple idiot, you think you can buy eternity with contortions! You're confusing the body with the biceps of a carnival wrestler! You're the perfect sucker for the patter of a charlatan! All those somersaults won't turn you into a saint!'

As usual, Zhuang fought against the hell of beliefs by telling a fable: A man wanted to be holy. He shut himself up in a cave to escape from the problems of the world. He meditated all day long, trying hard to create silence in himself but in reality, he only succeeded in falling into a state of total stupor. He ate only boiled nettles, bent his body, like a penitent, and paid no heed to the growl of his stomach. When he thought he had attained saintliness, he allowed himself to stick his nose outside. A tiger sprang out of the jungle and devoured him in a mouthful. 'He would have done better to live,' said Zhuang.

Zhuang made fun of his disciples and called them a disgusting bunch of sheep. He gathered a few of them around a big earthenware jar of wine so they could remember this amusing, exemplary story and learn from it:

'A father advised his son to imitate his Master and model his conduct after him. The son participated at a dinner next to his Master and did his best to eat like him, chew like him, drink at the same time he did, and imitate his slightest gesture. When he saw this little game, the Master burst out laughing, hiccupped, and threw up his millet cereal. The pupil tried to vomit by sticking a finger in his mouth but did not succeed. He bowed very low to his Master: 'Alas, I could not imitate your last, subtle action.'

The audience doubled up with laughter; some laughed so hard they cried and struck the ground with their fists. Up there on the mountain, caravan drivers heard them laughing and quickened their pace, thinking demons were living on the summits above the fogs.

CHAPTER TWENTY-NINE

The Ordinary Tao

We were a century before the invention of chopsticks, noodles and Taoism. The notion of Tao was not yet sacred. This word changed meaning with every sentence and its thousand possible nuances made it sparkle still more. It could signify the essence of everything, the door, the way, the method, the march forward, mastery, vital force, the act or the functioning of things. Of course, this short, sonorous word intrigued the disciples, as later on, it would be the supreme joy of the Taoist monks who would bow down before it. For Zhuang, the word was merely convenient. However, his disciple, Pei, who had disproportionately big ears, wondered about the one correct translation of the word. He cheerfully presented himself in front of Zhuang's cabin and addressed him unhesitatingly while the Master was admiring the bees coming and going on the stamens of flowers to gorge themselves on pollen.

'Master, I've found it!'

'Who are you?' grumbled Zhuang, disturbed in his observations.

'Don't you recognize me?'

'No.'

'I'm one of your most fervent disciples.'

'Fervour fatigues me.'

'You call me Pei-the-Parrot.'

'I must have seen into you clearly the day I gave you that nickname.'

'Remember, Master,' Pei-the-Parrot said, as if he had a fire inside him, 'Last year, I asked you "What is Tao?" and you struck me with your fan and chased me away. You wanted me to find the answer to my question by myself.'

'Well?'

'Well, I finally found it, Master!'

'Really?'

'Ask me the question again, Master!'

'What is Tao?'

'It is Tao.'

'Chatterbox!'

CHAPTER THIRTY

The Part of Heaven

Zhuang was growing old. The hairs in his beard were becoming hard and unruly. His beard had grown bushy now, and his thick eyebrows pointed up to the left and down to the right. He was neglecting himself as he aged, and he looked terrible. Was that the reason, or was it because he was so terribly demanding that when the towns and villages had to be rebuilt at the end of many wars, several of his first disciples had returned to the valley? Others had replaced them, attracted by rumours about the Master's reputation. This last wave was more encouraging, more open and knowledgeable. As the years went by, there were now a dozen of them surrounding Zhuang who had initiated talks where everyone gave their opinion. The Master would develop their argument or correct them. He had his favourite, named Lin Lei, and through his questions, he helped Zhuang clarify his ideas.

'Master,' he would say, 'You've been teaching us that tradition is barbarous . . .'

'It is tradition that feeds wars, tradition that forces men to do gruelling jobs, tradition that widens the gap between the rich and the poor, and it's tradition again that invents cults to divide men. Isn't that barbarous?'

'What exactly do you mean by tradition?'

'Rules of life, laid down by who knows whom or by some wicked divinity with a toad's head. People get used to them, believe in them and apply them without ever calling them into question. No one stands up and says "This rule is stupid"! I'll give you an example. One day, some sect decides that one must not eat pumpkins. So pumpkins are banished. They even frighten the members of the sect. 'You ate a mouthful of pumpkin? Poor you! You will die in horrible pain! Quick, spit it out while there is still time and swear you'll never do it again!' Now imagine a group of pumpkin worshippers on the other side of the river. What are they going to do? Will they cross the river to chop up whoever thinks pumpkin is the absolute evil? Probably. Wars have no other origin. Everyone remains locked into his beliefs that go against the beliefs of his neighbour. Don't you think it's stupid?'

'Stupid, Master, but deadly, too.'

'Oh yes, Lin Lei. I urge all of you to study what all those sects are advocating—they recognize each other by what they forbid. Amongst themselves, they call each other brothers. They reject everyone else. This hatred for pumpkins shared by one group may be due to indigestion, but then those stomach aches feed a belief, and the belief gives birth to still greater ills. Tse Lu, go pick a pumpkin for us!'

They often set out on an expedition far into the mountain on mule back, since Zhuang's strides were becoming shorter and long hikes tired his knees. On the way, the Master would point out medicinal plants and pick figworts for his bones, Scottish pine for his breathing and hawthorn for his heart. When they returned, loaded with fresh plants, they let their mules plod on without guiding them because the animals instinctively knew the way back. This allowed Zhuang to praise the natural virtues of animals:

'These mules are closer to Heaven than human beings.'

'How so, Master?'

'Men used to be part of nature, but they moved away from it when they came into close contact with each other. They became sociable, predictable, they turned into speech-makers. They weren't able to give free rein to their intuitions and refused to get rid of their fabricated reasoning, which stiffens reality.'

'Have we lost our natural faculties, then?' Lin Lei asked.

'When you hack down a venerable tree trunk in order to carve a vase out of it and decorate it in lively colours, you leave a heap of chips on the ground. The vase is superb, the shavings, negligible, and only good for burning. However, neither one resembles the original trunk any more. They have lost their original core. Similarly with men—the scoundrels and the virtuous have both lost their original essence.'

'But what makes us lose our natural faculties, Master?'

'Our abuse of the five senses.'

Zhuang clarified his formulation. There were five ways, he said, to lose our natural faculties; they are linked to our senses. Too many colours blur our vision, too many harmonious notes wear out our ears, too many perfumes ruin our sense of smell, too many flavours spoil our taste, too much touching turns into passion and leads our hearts astray.

'Moreover, these five factors I've briefly described are harmful to our health.'

The next day, as they were picking beans bent over their vegetable garden, Zhuang's back began to hurt.

'Take a rest, Master.'

'I'm not tired, I'm worn out, yes, worn out, but in good spirits.'

Tse Lu made him sit on a rock and massaged his back.

'The blood's still circulating,' Zhuang said, jokingly. 'When it wants to stop flowing, I will know, but I'm not completely rotten yet, my friend. Besides, when I look at you, I see you're not getting any younger— your hair is already turning grey. If I forget I'm alive, I don't know what the end will be. Life, you know, is a tumour, death is merely a burst abscess. Let's think of the beans we're gathering instead. They'll be delicious cooked in the fat of the goose we devoured the day before yesterday . . .'

Zhuang could still use his legs and wanted to prove it even if his left knee hindered him, so he went along with his friends who were going fishing in the little stream down below. Some mountain women and their children waved at them. One of them had a young urchin strapped on her back; she set him down on the ground and he immediately fell on his bottom. Another woman stood him up again, holding him by the arms; he tried a few steps before falling again. He was learning to keep his balance and moved his hands forward like balancing poles. Zhuang pointed at the scene with his bamboo cane:

'Look at that kid. He's taking his first steps. He ventures to put one leg in front of the other, he staggers, falls, gets up again, and hesitantly, starts over. He's conscious of his effort to keep standing.

When he loses that awareness, he will walk. He won't have any problems with balance because he has assimilated the mechanics of walking. Truly, the body never ceases to surprise me. The body is our master. That little one will walk by losing the awareness of walking. He won't have to make any effort, he will master the action of walking without even thinking about it.'

'You mean, Master, that we must lose our consciousness to solve many problems?'

'You can translate it like that . . .'

Zhuang explained that there were several levels of consciousness and reality was a constant metamorphosis. We had to embrace it as it was, without prejudices, without learned constructions, and forget oneself like that child as soon as he learns to move forward on his legs.

'That's the way it is for our daily movements—we pay no attention to them. We must reconnect with the force of nature within ourselves.'

'And reject thought?'

'Above all! Thought is artificial and numbs us. The body is stronger than the mind. The mind! Can you row forward if your boat is not in the water?'

The others were filling a big reed bucket with fish. The mountain women on the other bank were singing a melancholy tune. Zhuang added:

'Drive away idle questions. Listen to carefree people—without worries or misfortunes, they are empty.'

Over the next few days, Zhuang spoke again about the different levels of consciousness and how to go from all that is human to Heaven. His disciples did not understand everything he was saying.

It was clear from their pensive faces and even from their quickly stifled yawns.

'You can't tell when consciousness disappears,' Zhuang said. You can't see yourself falling asleep. And when we're dreaming, where are we? In reality or in illusion? Is reality truly real or is it a simple construct of the mind? And what about you—are you men or ghosts?'

Sensing that his disciples were baffled and had trouble following him—as so much of what he was saying went against their education—Zhuang suddenly got up and left them without a word to take a piss into the grass at the edge of the forest. Then, when he had satisfied his need, he turned around towards the little troupe that was scattering off:

'Tse Lu!'

'Master?'

'Come here! Tell me, I've often caught our friend, Lin Lei, frantically scribbling away in the pavilion. What's he writing? Do you know?'

'I can guess, Master.'

'So what do you guess, you stubborn old mule?'

'I think he's writing down your words while they're fresh in his mind—that's why he's in such a hurry.'

'But why?'

'To bear witness.'

'Oh, witnesses! Most of the time their testimony is all wrong. True, Lin Lei is the smartest one of the group, but I'm sure he waters down what I say. He'll make me say anything at all!'

From that day on, as he had no wish to be betrayed by someone close to him, Zhuang resolved to write. First, he wanted to gather, in few words, his perception of reality, of illusion, and the troubling line between the two. As soon as he had his brush in hand, a shamanic vision of the soul escaping from the body during sleep in the form of a butterfly rose in his mind. The butterfly was that god of sleep who came out through the nose of sleepers. Zhuang rubbed his brush on the ink stick. He was staging himself. Now he was dreaming. He was a butterfly gathering pollen from flower to flower when he suddenly woke up: 'Was it Zhuang Zhou dreaming he was a butterfly or a butterfly dreaming it was Zhuang Zhou?' From then on, he spent whole days in the Writing Pavilion. He only stopped at night after he had covered a great many bamboo cards. He would then dine with a hearty appetite and fall asleep in his cabin, taking up his interrupted dream again.

CHAPTER THIRTY-ONE

Last Words

With a totally independent mind, Zhuang was composing a book of universal wisdom which took his name: the Zhuangzi. He wrote out in his own hand the first seven chapters in a highly personal, bold tone. He made wild associations between mythological figures and lame craftsmen, scabby people, cripples, crooked faces and Chinese angels; he launched into lyrical flights, celebrated trees and giant birds, invented imaginary bearded men, disregarded chronology, resuscitated Confucius and put him into unflattering situations—but with gentle irony—distributed parts to characters that shed light on his own experiences. His style was dazzling, flamboyant, trivial, impulsive. After him, he suspected, his disciples would extend his text, trying to write in the same vein, and then the disciples of the disciples, but with less talent . . .

It did not matter.

Only the sun and the wind held him back now. He rose before the day to bless its appearance on the mountains, but he had trouble straightening up without leaning on a stick. 'Damn carcass!' he swore, insulting his pains and his rust. Some of his companions were hardly in better shape; he listened to them attentively and held forth on the normal passage of time: 'No present before the past, no end without a beginning, no grandchildren without children.' Tse Yu, who was nicknamed 'Scruffy' and was his age, took it up as a refrain: 'Life and death, appearance and disappearance, same thing.' They'd start laughing, but when Scruffy fell ill, Zhuang rushed to his cabin.

'What's wrong with you?'

'Old age!' Scruffy jested, raising himself up on one elbow. 'Don't you think it extraordinary that creation made me into this shapeless thing crumpled on a reed mat? Just look, my chin is falling towards my belly button, I have a bump on my shoulder blades, one of my shoulders is higher than my skull . . . Creation sure did a job on me!'

'Does that frighten you?'

'Not at all, Zhuang. Let creation turn my arm into a crossbow if it feels like it, I'll go shoot a quail and roast it!'

'You speak true. What has been lent to us can be taken back from us. Once we've understood how provisional things are, what is there to fear?'

'Still,' Scruffy said, 'After I die, I wouldn't really enjoy being reborn as a bedbug!'

They laughed so hard the red-beaked parrot that had landed on the windowsill took fright and flew off presto. Scruffy passed away the next day. He was buried beyond the squash patch. Zhuang drew a fine inscription on his grave: 'You split and dumped us, you old quitter!' Then he got drunk.

Gradually, Zhuang stopped living. His gestures were less precise, his footsteps shorter, his bushy eyebrows were like the brows of a theatre mask. He hollowed out from inside, his cheeks caved in, his protuberant bones outlined the shape of his skeleton. Soon, Tse Lu could pick him up like a handful of dry straw. As for him, he saw colourful planets turning and birds growing, losing their shapes and then becoming petals of fire.

'Master Zhuang, when your breath flies away, what would you prefer? Would you like to be buried under the earth or left alone with your face to the sky?'

'Whatever. If I'm buried I will delight the maggots. Exposed to the sun, I'll be the prey of vultures. Why favour one of those animals over the other?'

One morning, he had himself carried to the platform that overlooked the valley, leaving in his cabin everything he owned: a mat, a bowl and a statuette of white jade. He lay down on the fresh-smelling grass. He asked to be left alone and even the two little shrews that had ventured to sniff him understood. Zhuang closed his eyes and waited for death, which he sensed was imminent. It was a majestic day. He waited for hours without moving, perfectly calm. Towards evening, he felt a drop of water on his eyelid, another on his forehead. He groped around in the grass with his fingers, recovered his stick, grabbed it, got up, and scuttled over to take shelter in the Writing Pavilion.

'Damn rain!'

Paris, Hanoi, Trouville
March 2013–August 2014